RIVALS

For Emma, life was the curtain rising on the ballet stage each night—and trying to fill her empty hours with rehearsals and lovers.

For Deedee, life was the fulfillment of a husband and children—and the aching void of what she had never achieved.

For Emilia, Deedee's seventeen-year-old daughter, gifted with dancing genius and already initiated into the pleasures and betrayals of the flesh, life was facing the same choice both Deedee and Emma had confronted twenty years earlier—the discipline of a career or the hunger for love . . .

THE TURNING POINT
There is one in everybody's life.

Big Bestsellers from SIGNET

THE TURNING POINT

By

Arthur Laurents

A SIGNET BOOK

NEW AMERICAN LIBRARY

TIMES MIRROR

To Shirley Bernstein

SIGNET TRADEMARK REG. U.S. PAT. OFF. AND FOREIGN COUNTRIES
REGISTERED TRADEMARK—MARCA REGISTRADA
HECHO EN CHICAGO, U.S.A.

SIGNET, SIGNET CLASSICS, MENTOR, PLUME
and MERIDIAN BOOKS
are published by The New American Library, Inc.,
1301 Avenue of the Americas, New York, New York 10019

First Printing, November, 1977

1 2 3 4 5 6 7 8 9

PRINTED IN THE UNITED STATES OF AMERICA

Prelude

During the busy years, it was as though Deedee was looking through the wrong end of a telescope that grew longer and longer. The picture kept receding in memory, the figures grew smaller and less abrasive than life. Then Emma appeared again, and the telescope was unexpectedly flipped around. The figures became even larger than life, and the memory acquired a terrible power to hurt.

In the mirrored wall, each of them is executing the exact same movements, watching only herself. Michael is watching both of them, comparing, judging them as well as the choreography he is inventing. One of them will dance the leading role in this new ballet he is trying to shape.

Not an unusual scene, but the three figures in this picture are close friends, the two girls exceptionally so. They have been roommates since they joined the company four years ago at the age of eighteen. Their friendship began even earlier, over a pilfered bottle of champagne in Boston.

Both were dancers in a show that was lumbering through dress rehearsal on the eve of its out-of-town opening. In the fifties, ballet was obligatory for a Broadway musical, so they were not in the chorus: they were in the corps de ballet. It was their first and last show. It was also the first, though not the last, for the overbred producer. Intimidated by the choreographer-director, he allowed the rehearsal to stagger past midnight into expensive overtime. He sent out for sandwiches, beer and coffee for the company—and champagne for the principals.

Emma, whose calm seemed to conceal a fever, sipped water with her snack. Her feet propped on a chair, she sat against the wall in the farthest corner of the ballet girls' long dressing room. The sandwiches she had selected were placed on a white paper napkin next to her makeup, which was laid out on an immaculate white hand towel on the dressing table.

"Beer? I got an extra." Deedee, the one who was always open and cheerful, sounded and looked as though her day had just begun.

"I don't like beer, thank you." Like most dancers, Emma's voice was thin and flat. Her accent was Wilkes-Barre, Pennsylvania, but she was careful to speak very softly.

"Coffee?"

"It keeps me awake, thank you."

"Champagne?" Very offhand.

Emma stared in disbelief, but in two minutes Deedee was back with a bottle.

"Why not?" She giggled as she poured. "We're as talented as they are."

Emma tasted the champagne, then finished her glass. "We are," she said very seriously.

"You are."

"So are you."

They were sitting side by side at the long dressing table. Deedee looked shyly at Emma in the mirror.

"Really?"

"Yes. You just need to concentrate more."

Deedee refilled their glasses. "What're you going to do when we get back to New York?"

"Study."

"American Ballet's going to hold auditions."

"I thought they ran out of money."

"No. That lady in charge sold some more stocks or something. Let's audition, Emma!"

Emma carefully wiped the bottom of her glass. "You think we're ready?"

"What've we got to lose? This show isn't going to run. It's a turkey-lurkey," Deedee said grandly, repeating the phrase she'd overheard the costume designer use to the production secretary. (When the Boston reviews appeared, the costume designer was the first to be fired.)

"Thank you for the champagne," Emma said. And then, not looking at Deedee, said what she really wanted to say. "If you think I'm that good, why do you want me to audition with you?"

"Hey, I'm good!" Deedee laughed. "Besides, I want to have a friend when we both get in the company."

"You didn't have any friends when you got in this company. Now everybody's always in your room."

What struck Deedee at that moment was not that Emma had almost no sense of humor, but that Emma had no talent for friendship. Obviously she wanted it; yet, just as obviously, she was afraid of it, and held back. She wasn't alone there. Casual friends came running to Deedee, mistaking her directness for what she guessed they took as simple-mindedness. She welcomed their confessions and their company, but held herself in reserve for special people.

"I meant a best friend, Emma. Like back home."

Emma nodded, but her best, her only friend back home was her mother. It was months before she told Deedee about her.

"She teaches music in the high school. My father was always turning off the phonograph. When his company transferred him to Scranton, she said she couldn't go because of her job and my dancing teacher. So he went alone. I think he was relieved. I know she was.... I guess I was, too."

"Jesus! No wonder you have such concentration!" Deedee said. "In our house back in Dayton, you could never hear the phonograph because there were so many kids tromping in and out and yelling. I have three brothers, and it was my father who sent me to dancing school. He was afraid I was going to be a tomboy." She sat up straight. "You know, I never told that to anybody!"

"Why not?"

"Because I *am* a tomboy!" Deedee laughed, and then Emma smiled. A sense of humor was harder to develop than a friendship.

At twenty-two, after their four years with American Ballet—dancing in the corps together, becoming soloists together, always rooming together—they had never had a fight. Not even on the long, deadening tours where they played one-night stands, rode on cramped buses, danced on hard floors in smelly high-school gymnasiums, "ghosted" in sleazy hotels. "Ghosting" was stretching their artists' salaries by sleeping four or five or more in a double room. The two girls would register, then be assisted with a surprisingly large number of unmatching suitcases by other dancers. The sex of the ghosts didn't matter, not even to Emma. Michael was usually one, even after the moderate success of his first ballet.

It was when they were freezing in Milwaukee on the last tour that Deedee mentioned Wayne Rogers was going to ghost with them.

She tried to be casual—Wayne was a goal for everyone in the company, of all sexes—but her face got almost as red as her hair, her freckles showed, and her sea-blue eyes got even bluer.

Emma beamed: she had guessed right. "So that's why you've been helping him so much in rehearsals."

"What're you building? He's the perfect height to partner me. And he's very strong."

"Oh, you look very good together."

Deedee sighed. "He's so gorgeous, who couldn't look good with him?"

"You make him look better than he is."

"Come on! Wayne's very talented. Isn't he, Michael?"

Michael lit Emma's cigarette. "He's probably the nicest person in the company."

"But he's talented!" Deedee insisted. "What's 'nice' got to do with it?"

"He doesn't *want*," Michael explained. "And if you don't want, I'm not sure it matters how much talent you have."

"But I want!" Deedee cried. "Emma wants, you want. And we're nice, aren't we?"

The ballet they are rehearsing in the high-ceilinged room with the wall of mirror is based on *Anna Karenina*.

"Oh, Jesus!" Deedee moaned when Emma

told her. "Now I suppose we'll have to read the goddamn book."

They rarely glanced at a newspaper, their reason being that they were too busy taking class, rehearsing, performing; to relax, they ate a little and drank a lot after performances; no matter when they got home, and in what condition, they washed their tights and sometimes their hair; during the New York season, they were on Dexamil; and occasional sex was surely more necessary than a book. The previous year, there had been a rumor that Antony Tudor was going to do a ballet for the company, based on Proust. Deedee wailed and never got past the *madeleine;* Emma finished *Swann's Way*.

"A lot of good it did you," Deedee said. "Tudor canceled. Michael, are you positive?"

"Fairly." He rubbed his nose, which was like a Cocteau drawing. "I'd like to try both of you as Anna."

"Both?" they cried.

"I'm not exactly sure how I want to play her."

Leaning against the *barre* in front of the mirror, he still isn't sure, and the whole ballet centers on Anna. The story is fragmented, refracted through the lens of her whirling memory in those last moments before she throws herself under the train. She never leaves the stage, and so Michael is also watching Deedee and Emma to see how much physical stamina each has, where he must change his intricate patterns, how he can arrange resting places without relaxing the tension. Creation is agonizing for Michael. He works slowly, too often doubting himself, his material, his music, his dancers.

Each girl in the mirror is wearing old, soft pointe shoes, leg warmers, a beige leotard. Each now comes out of a perfect double pirouette with her hand rushing to smooth her hair; each executes the peculiarly Michael gesture the same way, yet each is a different Anna. Watching today, Michael sees with sudden clarity the two Annas he soon will have to choose between: Deedee's will be the victim of society and men, Emma's will be the victim of her own bottomless passion. He doubts whether ballet can support social commentary, but he fears romantic tragedy can too easily become hollow and sentimental.

Oddly, each girl's body seems better constructed for the other's Anna. Deedee is rounded, curved, womanly: rare among dancers, she has breasts that are visible and lovely. Yet, when she rises on pointe, she just escapes being too tall for most of the males in the company (Wayne is an exception); and her technique is so strong that even Dahkarova, the company's prima ballerina, watches her occasionally.

Emma is small enough for all partners but looks as tall as Deedee because of her long legs and her long, regal neck. She is thin, she is like a taut wire, yet when she dances, she seems without bones: even when she brushes her hair back in that tortured gesture, the movement is softly beautiful. But extraordinary power is always apparent, perhaps because of her intense concentration. This is centered in her face, a good face for the stage: very white, very black hair and eyes—really black velvet eyes—high cheekbones, and a broad pink mouth that is a surprise.

They are both tired. For a blur of weeks, they have been rehearsing the ballet in various cities but seemingly in the same mirrored room. It is still a long way from being finished, and Michael keeps changing much of what they thought was set.

He doesn't get the rehearsal time he needs; he is a new choreographer; also, he is not Balanchine, who has his own company. Still, he is not hurried by Adelaide Payton, who runs American Ballet, infusing it with her own money despite her New England husband and heritage. Adelaide conceals her thin steel frame with girlish ruffles and timid stoles. Although she murmurs, "Take your time, dearie," to Michael, to Emma and Deedee, her particular favorites for the future, she asks sharply, "But is it any good, dearie?"

No one is sure. Not Emma, not Deedee, certainly not Michael. Freddie Romoff, from Indiana, who is dancing Vronsky, Anna's lover, likes his pas de deux, but even Michael likes that: he has not changed it from the day it was set. Freddie prefers Emma as Anna, for she is smaller, easier to lift, and Freddie is afflicted with hangovers. Wayne, who is playing Anna's husband, prefers Deedee, of course. But the husband is a small part. Joe Rosenfeld, a big bear who dances in the pit while he conducts the orchestra, preferred Deedee from the beginning, but he just prefers Deedee and continues to prefer her, even though he knows Wayne has moved into Deedee's bedroom in the railroad flat she shares with Emma. Of course, a few weeks before the move, he opened a dressing-room door too quickly on Wayne and another boy. From what he saw, Rosie concluded it was not Wayne's first time. It wasn't, but Rosie mistook Wayne's enthusiasm for experience. Actually, much of Wayne's pleasure came from pleasuring others.

Rosie, who had lived in the ballet world for two years, assumed Deedee knew about Wayne, didn't care now, but would in time. He was half-right: Deedee knew, but she cared more than she would admit, even to Emma.

"So what? So they gossip. Jesus, they even gossip about you and me!"

"Really? What do they say?" Emma was amused.

"Ohhh, that we've done it."

"But they know we haven't."

"We almost did."

"When? Oh. Baltimore."

"Yes." Deedee laughed. "Saved by the bed-bugs! Anyway, I love Wayne, and God knows why, but he loves me."

"Yes, he does." Emma answered Deedee's unasked question. "Everybody wants him, but you've got him."

"I have, haven't I?" Suddenly Deedee was happy again. Even her feet stopped hurting.

Emma was one of the few who had never been after Wayne, partly because she was unable to pursue anyone, partly because her friendship with Deedee and her letters to her mother satisfied most of her few emotional needs. And partly because of Michael. Each recognizing some vague but satisfying limitation in the other, they had become lovers shortly after Deedee and Wayne fell in love. The affair might have lasted longer if they hadn't begun working on *Anna Karenina*.

"Does it bother you?" Michael asked one morning.

"What?" She got out of his bed.

"Well ... competing with Deedee, for one thing."

"No." She watched herself put up her hair in the mirror over his bureau. "Anyway, we don't think of it as competing. We dance the same role in lots of ballets."

The mirror was Chippendale, real. There was

little furniture, few objects in Michael's Village apartment, but it was all real.

"Does it bother you, Michael?"

"Not if it doesn't bother you. Or Deedee."

"Something does." No answer. "What, Michael?"

"Us." Although he wasn't thirty, and his body was both hard and lithe—he still danced with the company, mainly partnering Emma—Michael had deep lines running from his nose to the edges of his firm, sensual mouth. "We avoid saying things."

She began to put on her clothes. "If you're worrying about us," she said thoughtfully, "then you're thinking of me as Emma, not as Anna. That's bad for your ballet. So maybe we'd better stop this." She waved toward the bed.

He marveled at the unconscious grace of even that gesture. She misunderstood his smile.

"You're relieved, Michael."

"No, you are," he said.

They kissed and hurried to get the subway uptown to class and rehearsal, better friends than they had been before.

Michael moves away from the *barre* and watches them in the mirror again. It doesn't solve his problem. He doesn't know which Anna is better, which way the whole ballet should go, but he does know he must decide very soon. Next week, perhaps. He tells Emma and Deedee to rest, and has the pianist play the passage over again, just for him.

Panting, the girls turn away from the mirror and stretch their necks, press the small of their backs. They pick up their pastel sweaters, but Deedee, who is sweating far more than Emma, towels her face and neck first. She looks at their reflected figures and turns sideways to the mirror.

"I guess it's a good part," she says.

Emma shrugs. "Well, it's a long one."

"They don't come often."

"No. They don't."

"But if it's not good ... Is it, Emma? Really good? Is the ballet?"

They are almost whispering, and the piano is loud, but Emma can hear the strain in Deedee's voice.

"It could be weeks before we know for sure, Deedee."

"You know now. You always know!" The strain is visible now in Deedee's wet face.

"What's the matter with you today?"

Deedee hesitates, then grins, an imitation of herself. "Today isn't the matter. I have a bun in the oven."

Emma looks at Deedee's belly skeptically. "Are you sure? You know us." One of the many things they have in common is the irregularity of their periods.

"The doctor is. I'm three months gone."

Emma's eyes suddenly become opaque. Then she beams quickly, hugging her friend close. But Deedee cannot see her eyes.

"Oh, Deedee, it's wonderful!"

"Is it?"

"I'll bet Wayne—"

"He doesn't know. And I don't even know whether to tell him."

"Why not, for God's sake?"

"I don't want him to think he has to marry me."

"Oh, Deedee—"

"I don't have to have the baby."

Emma looks out the window. "If you don't, you'll lose him," she warns.

"Maybe, maybe not. But if I do have it, I'll lose the ballet, that's for sure."

"Ohh—" Emma's hand flicks away the ballet, "there'll be other ballets. What's important is you and Wayne. If you—"

But Michael is clapping his hands. "Come on, ladies," he says. "Back to Mother Russia."

"Later," Emma whispers to Deedee. She takes off her sweater and walks forward. Michael looks at Deedee. Hastily, she takes off her sweater and hurries forward. He looks at Emma and senses a new security, a confidence that makes him feel a bit more confident. Something has happened, but it does not concern Michael. His concern is his ballet.

"From the fives before the double pirouette," he says.

The pianist starts, and in the mirrored wall, each of the girls is again executing the exact same movements, watching only herself.

Chapter One

"You all ready? Everybody ready?"

Curlers in her new blondish-red hair, her new orange-and-brown chiffon grazing the floor, Dee-dee hurried out of the bedroom. One of her too-expensive new shoes pinched; she took it off and flexed it as she limped down the narrow hall to the kids' bathroom.

"Oh, gorgeous."

Ballet tights and a Little League baseball uniform dangled over the tub shower-curtain rail. She yanked them down, slammed them into the laundry hamper.

"Shit."

The new shoe had gone into the hamper. Fishing it out, she could almost hear the reeds running up and down scales as the orchestra tuned up and twirling figures warmed up nervously behind the house curtain. Silly; a sentimental fantasy of self-identification: they wouldn't be nervous about performing in Oklahoma City, certainly not Emma. She pulled and tugged at the tight shoe as though it, not time, was her enemy, and scurried into the living room.

Still tidy, and no one had been at the little bowls of potato chips and mixed nuts. It was a good room, it worked; at least, that was how she felt the few times she ever really thought about it. Now she looked it over anxiously, trying to see it as they would, particularly as Emma would. The mixture of overstuffed and faded with Mexican and colorful was a little slapdash but O.K., comfortable, inviting; the plants hanging from the beamed ceiling, filling the corners, punctuating the shelves in the bookcase—maybe too many, but healthy, and so green they had to be real; the framed ballet photographs, posters, programs—all right, they did crowd the white walls, but she wouldn't take one of them down. Anyway, they were all over the whole house, they were what made it *their* house, hers and Wayne's.

He was sitting on the couch, gently massaging Emilia's feet. Merely good-looking now, with pouches under his eyes, deep lines in his forehead, and the new white hairs in his sideburns that had made her suddenly kiss him just the other day. The new tie she had bought him was loose; the collar of his western shirt was open; his jacket sprawled across the back of the leather armchair. Maybe he'd keep the jacket buttoned over his beginnings of a beer belly during the party.

"I thought you were going to set up the bar," she said, annoyed by his calmness.

"There'll be plenty of time after we get back, honey." His Southwestern twang had returned when they settled in Oklahoma City.

"Oh, Wayne!"

She hobbled into the den without seeing him wink at Emilia, and Emilia smile back.

Her smile contradicted Emilia, making her look sixteen, not nineteen, even now with her hair gathered up ballerina fashion. It also made her seem as open and outgoing as her mother, whereas even Deedee often speculated what her oldest daughter was really thinking. The most radical effect of the smile, however, was on Emilia's eyes. Deep blue, much darker than Deedee's, they dominated her casually pretty face with an odd mixture of limpid sensuality and secret steel that was a challenge. When she smiled, the challenge vanished along with the mystery: she was just pretty. But she rarely smiled, and then it was usually for her father. Her adoration of Wayne was as obvious as Deedee's had been twenty years earlier. Too obvious, Deedee thought, but was careful not to say a word. Some boy would turn up, and that would be the end of that. Although Deedee didn't see how a boy good enough for Emilia could turn up in Oklahoma City. There was only one Wayne.

He had, of course, set up the bar in the den. He even had California wine chilling in the

Styrofoam cooler they used to take on picnics when the kids were little. Deedee wondered when she would stop marveling that Wayne not only saw through her, but accepted what he saw. He knew why she was irritable; by teasing about the bar, he'd been trying to say her anxiety was foolish. As full of resolution as New Year's, she put on her shoe and went back in the living room. Wayne was still massaging Emilia's feet. Emilia was almost purring.

"Put your shoes on, Emilia," she ordered, and, annoyed at herself, stormed into the kitchen.

Janina, her fifteen-year-old, was decorating platters of chicken salad and sliced ham with freshly washed sprigs of parsley. Her round, plain face had a seriousness that left people surprised she didn't wear glasses.

"There'll be plenty of time for that later," Deedee said. "Where's Ethan?"

"Those beads look absolutely gross with that dress."

"Emma gave them to me before you were born."

"They still look gross." Calmly Janina transferred the platters from the butcher-block island to the round table in what had been a dining room until Wayne knocked out the separating wall.

"Ethan!" Deedee rapped on the kitchen window, then slammed out the back door. "Ethan, you quit that!"

Her twelve-year-old was doing *tour jetés* across the grass in his sneakers. The grass, like everything else in the yard, was marvelously green. Poplars concealed the small lot from the neighbors and the street in back; at the base of the trees was a rim of bushes and shrubs and plants that the family took turns watering and fertilizing. The planting had been done for privacy, but it also sheltered the yard from the maddening hot wind that always blew across the city in spring. Even the little colored lights—their Christmas-tree lights—that Wayne had strung from the roof of the patio to the garage were scarcely swaying. Only Ethan moved, a homemade prince leaping for the colored stars in the last of twilight.

"Ethan, did you hear me?"

"It's the lights! I'm crazy!"

"The lights are for the party." Deedee switched them off. "You're going to be covered with sweat, and we have to leave in exactly five minutes!"

"You going with curlers in your hair?"

"Jesus!"

She dashed back into the air-conditioned house through the glass doors of the patio, and into her bedroom. Air-conditioning was one fact of Oklahoma City life that had become as natural as morning coffee. On it went in May, off in October. Cars, shops, offices, everything was air-conditioned. One millionairess even had an air-conditioned garden. The Rogers yard was a furnace in summer, but they watered doggedly every evening, and all the green looked so cool, they sometimes sat in the patio in August.

Curlers out, hair assembled and fluffed, Deedee surveyed herself in the oval pier glass, the one thing kept from Wayne's mother's house when she died. Everything else, even the cut glass and silver, had been sold, and the money, less than expected, plowed into the Rogers School of Ballet.

She was pleased with the hair, and the new dress hid the truth very attractively. Emma's beads *did* clash. Regretfully, she put them on the dresser next to a faded photograph of herself and Wayne in the Bluebird pas de deux. She peered at herself in the picture, then at her reflection. Eight pounds could go, but after forty, eight pounds less meant eight years more in the face and neck. She pulled up, held her stomach in: who was kidding who? She sagged, crumpled inside, fought tears.

"I can't go," she said to Wayne's reflection in the pier glass. "Look at me!"

He grinned over her shoulder and put his arms around her waist and kissed her neck. "I'm seventeen years older, too. We all are. Even Emma."

"But she's been taking class every day."

"You've been teaching class every day."

"Not the same."

"Thank God. You've got curves."

"So have you."

He laughed with her and hugged her tighter. "What the hell! We're still in the profession."

"Yeah. A ballet school in the dust bowl."

"Want to run an antique shop? Or would you rather raise poodles?"

Both were thinking of the same dancers, all the dancers they had known. Ballet trained you for nothing but ballet. You started too young, you finished too early, and when you were finished, you were really finished. Tendonitis, and nothing in the bank except your fare home.

"Can we get this show on the road, if you don't mind?" Ethan stood in the doorway, Emilia and Janina behind him.

"Get your butt in the car." But Deedee's voice was warm and affectionate. She watched the kids go, then turned to Wayne. "We've done pretty O.K.," she said proudly.

Deedee had lived in Oklahoma City for seventeen years without settling in. Wayne had been born there, but to her it was a city only because its name claimed it was. What she saw was a small town crouched over a big prairie, a more affluent Levittown of neat brick houses and characterless shopping malls marked out on an enormous flat of earth the color of dried blood. All the trimmed, flowerless yards, back and front, couldn't wipe out the gashes of that unloving red soil edging the highways she drove every day to and from the Rogers School of Ballet. Trees were a novelty, almost as much of a surprise as a ten-inch grade in a road. Flatness was endless, everywhere; it flattened the people.

They had chosen the section where they lived because they were told it had good public schools for the kids (meaning few blacks, they found out later). It was pleasant, middle-income, but nevertheless a pancake of tidy yards and brick houses whose color was a dull reminder of the earth they squatted on. (Even unflappable Wayne had been driven crazy by Deedee's refusal to live in a red-brick house. Finally they found one that was tannish-yellow. Still brick, though.) Their next-door neighbors, the Van Cleaves, worked on their yard in the evenings only: Mrs. chugging over the grass on a tiny tractor lawnmower, Mr. clipping and pruning the low hedge and guzzling Coors. The Van Cleaves had the arcane theory that garden surgery was fatal unless performed between sunset and moonrise. Otherwise, they were as flat as the rest of the neighbors.

"And as nice," Wayne said.

"What's nice?" Deedee asked. "Content enough to be agreeable? If they're so content, why do they drink so much?"

"Because it's a dry state." Wayne laughed.

Most of the people they met were contented and agreeable; they'd been born in Oklahoma, or the Southwest at any rate, and had stayed by choice. To them, Dallas and Las Vegas were

London and Paris, and their minds never traveled anywhere. Still, they were nice people;
over the years, their telephone numbers were
added to the Rogers address book; pleasant
people who regarded Deedee and Wayne as
friends because they saw them more or less reg-
ularly. Neighbors, parents of friends of their
kids, parents of kids who took ballet lessons.

The ballet parents lived mostly in Nichols
Hills, the best section in town. Many of their
big houses were all wood, some were painted
white, a few were contemporary; all had trees.
On weekends they flew to football games and
Neiman-Marcus, two or three in their own
planes. California was traditional for summer,
Colorado for winter; they discovered Mexico
and came home bearing tequila.

"Flat," Deedee commented.

One youngish Nichols Hills couple, the Fernbachers—really loaded, both their families in
oil—democratically invited Deedee and Wayne
to Saturday-night bashes, Sunday Puerto Val-
larte Mary brunches by the pool. Ken Fernbacher often brought his two little girls for
their ballet lesson himself and stayed to split a
beer with Wayne. He loved rodeos, looked like
a rodeo rider, reminisced with Wayne about rodeos they had gone to when they were kids.
Deedee suspected Wayne was why Ken Fernbacher kept inviting them over, but, a little
frightened and certainly ashamed of the suspicion, she only joked about it to Wayne.

There was a homosexual couple they occasionally exchanged dinners with. One ran the plant nursery on the shopping mall where they had their ballet school; his lover was a young doctor. Ballet brought them together. Not that the two fellows had any real interest in ballet: they simply and correctly assumed that two ex-dancers would accept them as a couple. And they wanted heterosexual friends. All four talked about plants and flu shots and inflation and how much everybody else drank and the ambitious reconstruction work going on downtown. They were pretty much like all the other couples Deedee and Wayne saw, except they couldn't be mixed with the others, limiting friendship with them, and friendship with the others.

Of course, they could be and were invited with a few people Deedee and Wayne knew in the Architecture Department of the university. The Architecture Department was traditionally bohemian, swinging, far-out—the description depended on the decade. Now it was once again swinging. But Deedee and Wayne weren't swingers; and the academic mind, whatever its insularity, was above their level. Their subject, what they really knew, what she really cared about, what she missed talking about, was ballet.

The closest they had come to real friends was when the Mummers opened a new theater with a professional company. Shorthand communication with the actors was almost immediate. They felt they were part of a family, almost as they had been in the ballet. Cousins maybe, but members; the town didn't look so flat. The Oklahomans, however, went to the theater once, to see if it really did look as though Rube Goldberg designed it. It did, and they didn't return. So, along with no dance, no music, there was no theater (even road shows of Broadway hits didn't do business in Oklahoma City). The Mummers became an amateur company. Deedee and Wayne went twice: the misplaced enthusiasm depressed them even more than the lack of technique and talent. They had no respect for the players, and therefore, no real friendship with them.

For Deedee, even though they knew faces and kept meeting more, they had no friends at all. Not friends as she and Emma had been. Even she and Michael. Occasionally there was a surprise card from Michael—wish-you-were-here in Tokyo, or Oakland. Well, he was artistic director of American Ballet now, as well as Famous Choreographer. Emma still wrote, less and less frequently, notes now, not letters. Still she always remembered her godchild: birthday and Christmas, there was a little package for Emilia from some glamour store, usually in New York, but often in London, Paris, Rio, cities Deedee had never gotten to. She kept a scrapbook of Emma, which Emilia had taken over: reviews, articles, pictures from dance magazines, glamour magazines, news magazines, even the covers. Two books on Emma were on the shelf in the bedroom Emilia shared with Janina. Lately, however, there were fewer articles, fewer pictures. The last pages of the scrapbook were empty, waiting, like Deedee, for Emma to appear. She had never had a friend like Emma.

In the early years, it hadn't mattered. She hadn't time to miss friends, scarcely had time to answer Emma's letters. She was too busy having and raising her children, helping the school get going, enjoying her love for Wayne, delighting in their intense sexuality. But passion dwindled, naturally, and simmered down: sex was occasionally more than merely O.K., but sporadic. The school was established, financially they could breathe; in the last couple of years, she had begun to realize that in another two or three years, the kids would be going, going, gone. And she was over forty. Almost half her life had been spent in the ballet, had been lived in that special, private, insulated world. Now she had begun to miss it like a family. Teaching klutzy kids, few of whom really wanted to become dancers and even fewer who could, was no longer enough. Wayne was her friend, but one friend from that world, her world, was no longer enough. She loved him and her kids, but they were no longer enough. Nothing was any longer enough. She even began to wonder whether it ever had been. Looking back became dangerous.

For Wayne, it was enough. His closet in their bedroom was full of the western-cut clothes he had yearned for as a boy. In the drawers in his half of their big dresser, his side of their desk, everything was in its proper place. He didn't want to open a drawer and be surprised, and never was. Those other drawers of desires and ambitions he'd left home to open had been firmly shut since his return; he had neither wish nor need to open them again. He had been relieved to come home to the flat land that was as familiar and welcome as the flat people and their "hi, y'all" friendship. In the ballet, the intimacy, the intensity of friendship had been a problem for him; back in Oklahoma City, he had expected being a ballet teacher to be a problem. But having a wife and three children had helped, and he was, after all, a native son.

He had loved being part of the ballet company, particularly after he'd married Deedee. They had stayed for more than a year after Emilia was born. It had been six months before Deedee could dance again, and then she wasn't quite as good as she had been. Probably because she had to take it easy. Anyway, touring with a baby was impossible, physically and financially. It was no way to raise a child, and by then he knew he wanted more children. He loved kids, which was probably why he was a better teacher than Deedee. She was only at her best if they had some talent. He enjoyed all of them, was patient with all of them, encouraged all of them. He wanted all of them, good, bad, indifferent, to learn how to use and enjoy their bodies. He did most of the teaching; Deedee did all of the paperwork.

Recently Wayne had begun to drink a little too much because Deedee did, and because he suspected why she did. Their late-night talks stuttered with silence. Nevertheless she wouldn't let him turn on the television except for a special program; she refused adamantly to become an addict. Because even with the silences, even without drinks, when they sat together in the den she felt safe. Safe from what, she didn't stop to analyze; probably safe from a residue of a past that was an increasing threat to today and tomorrow.

The letter from Emma saying that American Ballet was finally coming to Oklahoma City, deliriously welcome as it was, made her heart quicken with fear that her safety was in danger. Or was it a fear of seeing Emma again after so many years? The picture of the figures in the mirror popped up with startling clarity as she busied herself with preparations for her party for the company. She decided not to have any neighbors, parents, outsiders: just family, the ballet family.

Now, walking into the huge old auditorium still called the Music Hall, she wondered whether that had been such a good idea. So many years later! How many dancers were left in the company whom she and Wayne still knew? He nudged her, and she waved and smiled hello as they made their way down the aisle. She had sent a blanket invitation to the whole company, but how many would really show? And what could she talk about? The orchestra was tuning up; the house was filling, almost sold out in the orchestra. For *her* company. Oh, she wanted them to be good!

She took the souvenir program Wayne handed her and flipped through it until she came to a full-page photograph of Emma. As Anna Karenina. She stared at it, seeing instead the reflections of herself and Emma in that mirrored wall, watching herself turn sideways to examine the outline of her belly in the mirror. The lights went out, there was applause for the conductor, and she applauded, too. *Anna Karenina* was the last ballet on the program. She didn't know how she was going to sit through the others.

Pale silver light barely revealed the stage for the opening ballet, *La Bayadère*. In a corner far at the back, a hazy shaft of silver began to glow around a lovely young girl in a long white gossamer tutu as she floated down a misty incline. Another young girl appeared behind her, floating in the same way; then another and another and another. Deedee floated with them. Her first important role with American Ballet had been that of the first girl in *Bayadère*. It was very hard, it required enormous control: the movements had to be phrased precisely to the music, because all the girls, the entire corps de ballet, flowed down the ramp, winding back and forth across the stage, timing their steps, the same steps repeated over and over, to the pattern set by the first girl. *Had* she been the first girl that first time? Or had it been Emma? They had alternated, that she remembered, but which of them had followed the other that very first time?

Next to her, Emilia leaned forward. Sevilla Haslam was on stage. Adelaide always had a foreign prima ballerina. This one was English, the style was unmistakable. Wayne winked at Deedee. She had always called the English ballerinas Bird Ladies. Delicately graceful, with skinny birdlike arms and legs, and the ability to take lyrical wing in the air. But she always waited for them to twitter and coo. Sevilla was really good, one of the best. How had Emma felt when Sevilla came into the company?

"Wow!" It was Ethan. Even Janina stopped fiddling with her program. The entire audience was electrically still, focused on Yuri Kopeikine, the latest Russian defector from the Kirov Ballet to be called the greatest male dancer in the world. If he wasn't yet, he would be in time. Even in the brief life span of dancers, Yuri had plenty of time: he was only twenty-five. With the hard, compact body of a gymnast, the coarse handsomeness of a Slavic peasant, he danced like the most lyrically elegant of princes. Even the Oklahomans knew they were seeing something extraordinary: a superathlete, an acrobatic magician who could take off like a Piper Cub and spin and twist and roll before he decided to land. Hey, was this ballet?

It was, but only Deedee and Wayne and Emilia and Ethan fully understood why. Even Janina only half-appreciated the beauty of Yuri's musical phrasing, the power that made the difficult seem effortless, the acting that gave meaning to movement.

"Nobody can compete with that!" Deedee said in the intermission.

"Emma won't have to." Wayne put his arm around her. "There're two ballets before *Anna*."

"And it's mainly acting."

"Oh, there are some difficult passages."

"I wonder if she can still do them."

He looked at her. She opened her program and flipped the pages. "Freddie Romoff's still doing Vronsky. Who's this joker doing your part?"

Wayne grinned. "Doesn't matter. It wasn't much of a part."

"It was when you did it!" she said fiercely. Her face was very white.

"Come on!" Emilia tugged at Wayne. "I don't want to miss one minute!"

To Wayne's surprise, when the curtain rose on Emma as Anna Karenina, the audience applauded. Deedee didn't hear the applause. The shock of seeing Emma made her deaf; the impact made her unaware of anything except that hypnotic figure on the stage. Something had happened: the promise of twenty years ago had been fulfilled; Emma had grown into her face, her body; she was a stark beauty. She moved with the assurance of a superb sorceress. Her concentration was so developed now, so intense, that she seemed to have a huge spotlight burning inside her. There was no one else on stage, no one else to see, no one else to care about as they cared about Emma's Anna. As she made them care, even made Deedee care.

Part of Deedee, anyway. In a great speaking actress, that burning light might have blinded her to the fact that Emma was too old to play Anna. In a great dancing actress, no light, however dazzling, could blind anyone who knew ballet as well as Deedee did, who knew that role as well as she did, to the plain fact that Emma was too old to dance. The risks she once took, which every dancer *had* to take, she was subtly careful not to take now. Oh, she hid her caution, but Deedee saw it.

Or did she? Was she seeing what she wanted to see, or what was there? The mirror image of those two figures executing exactly the same movements was looming larger, coming between her and the stage. That half-circle of piquet turns—hadn't it been a full circle originally? And faster? Ah, but Anna's dizzying torment was so painful, what did steps matter? Emma's hands went to her hair in that agonizing, peculiarly Michael gesture—did Deedee touch her hair? Or was that the Deedee in the mirrored wall? Had Emma done a double pirouette or a single? Had she fallen off pointe? Deedee wasn't sure, couldn't see, didn't know that tears were blurring her eyes, didn't hear her breath come in gasps, didn't feel Wayne touch her arm.

During the calls, when Freddie stepped back and Emma bowed and bowed alone in the spotlight before the house curtain, the audience cheered. Deedee heard Emilia cheering, smiled at her to show she was happy, and tried to cheer herself. Nothing came out; she was choking. Still smiling, she made her way past Emilia, out of the row, up the aisle, then swiftly down the stairs to the lounge, ran into the ladies' room, into a cubicle, where she slammed the door and locked it and was no longer choking because the sobs were coming out and the tears were streaming down her face as she stood with her head and the flat of her hands pressed hard against the cold white metal wall. She let herself go, unable to stop the tears that might have been for what she was now or for what she had never been and never could be anymore.

In the lounge, Wayne waited patiently, a paper cup from the water fountain in one hand, a tiny airliner-size bottle of brandy in the other:

he'd come prepared. When she finally came out, she looked better than he'd figured. She'd bathed her eyes with cold water, repaired most of the damage. Emma would've expected her to cry anyway. He grinned at her rueful grimace, filled the cup, and handed it to her. She downed the brandy gratefully.

"What'd you say to the kids?"

"Nothing. I didn't have to." He took the paper cup and dropped it in a waste bin. "They know you, and they've heard the saga of you and Emma rehearsing for *Anna* a hundred times."

As they started up the stairs to the lobby, she asked, "What'd you think of her? I don't mean her performance. That's pure Emma, and it's still incredible. Her dancing."

"All things considered, good."

"Really?"

He hesitated. "O.K. She'd be better off if she cut some of the stuff that's too difficult for her now. Satisfied?"

"You make me feel like the Wicked Witch. Which I guess I am."

"About Emma you are." He stopped abruptly. She turned to him, her back to the staircase wall. "For Chrissake, Deedee, are you hung up over something that happened twenty years ago?"

"I thought I'd forgotten it."

"Well, you haven't!" Relenting, he kissed her, "Do me a favor?"

"Sure."

"Get rid of it. Talk to her."

Deedee nodded, but as they started up the stairs again, she said, "I don't know what she's like now."

Inside the unfamiliar stage entrance, they hung back, hesitant to push on to what, in another life, had been home; afraid they would be as unrecognized as the other visitors clutching programs, waiting for autographs; nervous they would be exposed and demeaned before their children. The kids, including Janina, gaped at the young dancers (were we ever that young? Deedee wondered), some in costume, some in street clothes, running in and out of dressing rooms, up and down stairs. Half-caught sentences:

A pretty, dark girl: "Only steak and yogurt."

"I don't care how much you can lose, Sandra, it's too expensive."

"But yogurt's so great for the skin, it's like saving money."

Wayne shook his head at Deedee: still money problems. Did they still "ghost"? (They did.)

"It wasn't a cramp, it's tendonitis."

"Pity. I wonder who'll take over the part."

That, apparently, was eternal.

"How're you getting to the party?"

"Are you well? I'm doing the bars—and there're four of 'em!"

That also, apparently, was eternal.

"But they adore you, Sevilla!" Yuri's English was surprising for the short time he had been in the country. Or perhaps the sentence was universal. Limping slightly, he followed Sevilla, who was dressed for Fifth Avenue.

"Oh, Yuri, they loved everybody. They're absolute idiots." Clutching a bouquet in one hand, she stopped to paw her purse with the other for a cigarette for the long holder clamped between her teeth. Emilia stared at her; Ethan gaped at Yuri, who took the purse, found the cigarette and a lighter, as Sevilla nattered on.

"What is the point of devoting one's whole bloody life to achieving a perfect arabesque for an audience that doesn't know the difference? I was ghastly tonight, and they thought I was fantastic." She exhaled like a smokestack. "Spare me the provinces." She snapped her bag shut. "I'm going straight to my hotel and soak in a hot bath."

Deedee timidly blocked Sevilla's exit. "Excuse me, Miss Haslam. I'm Deedee Rogers. My husband, Wayne? It'd make us so happy if you—"

"Of course." Sevilla smiled as she had trained herself to do in hundreds of theaters and reached for Deedee's souvenir program. "I'm afraid I don't have a pen...."

"Oh, what I meant was that we're giving the—"

"Pencil do?" Wayne stuck the pencil in Sevilla's hand and held out his program. She signed with a flourish and swept out the stage door.

Yuri smiled at Deedee. "I bring guitar to party?"

"Oh, please!"

"How's the knee?" Wayne asked him as one dancer to another, sounding more like osteopath to patient.

"Broken." Yuri grinned. Snaring a pretty Eurasian ballet girl, he leaned heavily on her and was starting back toward his dressing room when Ethan suddenly reached out and shook Yuri's free hand.

"You're great," he muttered.

"So are you," Yuri said solemnly.

Ethan blushed happily and hid his face against Janina.

Deedee and Wayne felt better, easier, wonderful: one of the world's greatest dancers was coming to *their* party, complete with girl and guitar! They *were* home as they moved confidently toward the wings, looking around for faces; not the young, the new, but the familiar—what the hell, the old faces—the members of their old family.

"Jesus God, Wayne! Deedee!" It wasn't dashing, arrogant Vronsky, but Freddie Romoff, aging worse than they, sweat and strain crumbling the face he hadn't yet removed. His bathrobe was bleary with the makeup of a thousand performances. It dated back to days he and Wayne had shared a dressing room: Freddie was superstitious.

They rushed into each other's arms, all three at once. Not wanting to look openly at what the years had done, and suddenly not caring, either. Hugging, kissing, laughing, talking without listening, the words tumbling into their embraces. Then another dancer called out from the past; another cried instantly; another and another; character dancers now, mimes, small-part people grateful nevertheless to belong and be paid. Old friends holding on to Deedee and Wayne as though they could hold on to the past; welcoming them home, back home with the family.

Over their shoulders, Deedee searched for Emma, wanting to see her for one moment before Emma saw her. A lesser memory materialized and interrupted; Adelaide Payton, still living for her American Ballet company. Mottled gray-white now, her long hair was still tied back with that girlish velvet ribbon; another girlishly ruffled dress hung from her scarecrow frame. But her back was ramrod straight even as she twittered to the squat, heavy-breasted lighting woman. Nearby, the company manager waited impatiently, the statement of the night's receipts in his hand. He was young, he was new; he wore a sports jacket. Turning to him, Adelaide saw Deedee.

"Hello, dearie." As though no time had

elapsed. Well, maybe rape could surprise Adelaide. "You've held up quite well."

"So have you."

"Running the company keeps me trim. You could lose a few pounds."

Deedee laughed. "So you always said."

Adelaide looked back through the years. Abruptly she kissed Deedee, then just as abruptly released her.

"No cake or candy tonight, I hope."

"Not a cookie, cookie." Deedee smiled, but Adelaide already had the box-office statement in hand. Deedee moved slowly into the wings. She let her fingers remember the feel of the black velvet legs, looked down at a rosin box, and let one of her new shoes rub back and forth in the rosin.

"Deedee!"

A distinguished bald man with a heavily furrowed face and a handsomely trimmed white beard. A striped blue suit buttoned over his thickened waist. He removed his gold-rimmed eyeglasses.

"Deedee, it's Michael."

Michael, with his long black hair and young, clear eyes watching her and Emma in the mirror. Michael, with his reedlike body, his muscular legs in sleek tights flying across a stage to meet Emma and lift her high in the air.

"Oh, Michael! Wayne, it's Michael! Michael's here!" She hugged him, felt the softness, the flabbiness, and hugged him tighter; let him go so he and Wayne could hug each other, then just stand smiling so fondly at one another.

"My God, you look impressive!" Wayne said.

"So impressive Deedee didn't recognize me."

Embarrassed, she laughed and kissed him again. "Well, you weren't the great choreographer when we left the company."

"Wasn't I? I thought I was."

"You'd only done *Anna*."

There had always been something removed about Michael. He looked directly at you when he was talking to you, he listened, but a part of him was often in another room. Now Deedee saw herself come sharply into focus in his eyes.

"Out there." He pushed her gently out on the stage.

The backdrop for his ballet was still in place, attempts to paint away its age exposed by the flat work lights. Emma stood in front of it, singing a passage from the score to the conductor, her graceful hands conducting the tempo she wanted. She was warmly wrapped in a beautifully tailored dressing gown; she had taken off her wig but not her makeup. Watching, Deedee wondered whether Emma knew she was there, was performing consciously, was as nervous as she was.

The conductor thanked Emma extravagantly, and she looked around. She hadn't known Deedee was there. A smile broke across her face, and, both hands reaching out, she came swiftly across the stage.

"Here you are!"

Deedee smiled, but she wasn't sure who this woman was. The extreme ballet makeup was like a mask on top of another mask. It couldn't hide her beauty, a beauty Deedee lacked, any more than it could hide the fact that although they were the same age, Emma looked older, a good deal older. Her voice was low, throaty now. Pennsylvania was gone; her accent was right for a woman who had been presented to royalty, who dined at embassies, who had been a ballerina for a long time, not only on stage, but off.

They embraced quickly, gingerly, like women at lunch, and began babbling desperately.

"Oh, Emma, you were marvelous!"

"No, but I wanted to be."

"You were!"

"My foot's acting up. I wrote you about the fracture—"

"I couldn't tell, honestly—"

"Thank you for the flowers. I was so nervous because you were here—"

"It didn't show, you were marvelous."

"You really were, Emma." Wayne joined them in time. They were beginning to drown in the flood of their own meaningless words. "You moved me, just as you always did."

"Oh, Wayne." Emma embraced him freely. "It's been too long!"

More smiles, smiles all around. Then Wayne

broke the awkward silence. "Hey! How do you like your godchild?"

At the edge of the wings, Emilia had been watching quietly, Ethan and Janina half-hiding behind her. Shyly she walked over.

"The last time I saw you," Emma said, "I could still pick you up." She turned to Deedee. "She's lovely."

"Yes," Deedee said, "she is."

The other kids were inching their way forward.

"And this is Janina," Emma said, "and—"

"Ethan," Ethan said firmly.

"Ethan. Of course." Emma smiled brightly. "Well! Look at all of you!" She held the smile for each of the children, their father, their mother. "They don't know how fast time goes, do they?" she said to her old friend, and she had lost her smile.

"No," Deedee said softly, "they don't."

"Oh, Deedee." Emma's voice trembled. Suddenly then, the only mask was the familiar ballet makeup they both used to wear, and it was her best friend Emma who had begun to cry, too.

"It's all right," Deedee said. "Really. It's all right."

They reached out blindly, put their arms around each other, holding on tightly to keep the years from coming between them.

Chapter Two

Wayne went on ahead with the kids, leaving Deedee and Emma to chatter away in the dressing room, even while Emma was in the shower. When she came out, Deedee marveled and envied her body.

"Jesus! I'll bet you don't weigh a hundred wet."

"The thighs are the problem."

"Well, you're never going to see mine again. Or my ass!"

Unconsciously Deedee smoothed her dress over her large, still-lovely breasts. In the dressing-table mirror, Emma saw, and began to dress with more speed than usual. Then she sat down and got to the real work: her face and hair. Her makeup looked as if it had just been set out on the white linen hand towel. Four or five little photographs in odd antique frames made the table less impersonal: home, even for two nights.

"Still disgustingly neat." Deedee inched closer, drawn by the magnet of the past to the dressing table, to sit at the place next to Emma as she used to. "I was a total slob, wasn't I?"

"Only when you borrowed my eye liner and didn't return it."

"To its proper place." She squinted at one of the snapshots, then held it up to the light. "Oh, Emma! You don't cart this everywhere you go?"

"That"—Emma pointed to another frame— "and Mother. The others appear and then disappear into the scrapbook."

Deedee shook her head at the snapshot in disgust. "Did I really wear that hat to my own wedding?"

"Can you believe how young we looked?"

"I look like shit."

"Next to Wayne, we all do. Wasn't he beautiful?"

"Even in pleated pants." Deedee returned the picture to its place. "Well, thank God your eye was elsewhere."

"You mean on Michael?"

"No: on the ball."

Their eyes met in the mirror; carefully, they smiled. Deedee watched Emma put on a pair of small diamond earrings. The cost of the earrings, that dress, those matching shoes, was more than the Rogers School of Ballet made in a month. Two months.

"What's it like to be you now, Emma?"

"I don't know. I invented whatever it is I am." Emma laughed evasively. "After I did

Anna, I knew I would get there. But I knew the rest of me had to get there too, and I didn't know where to begin. Then, one night, Dahkarova came by—it was right after Adelaide had eased her out of the company. She said"— Emma did a very good imitation of the old Russian ballerina's accent—" 'For ballerina, you must take every penny of salary and put it on your back—in black.' " She laughed again, then saw Deedee's polite smile in the mirror and shrugged. "I'm just talking." She began to brush her hair briskly. It helped keep her voice casual. "What's it like? I dance, Deedee. I take class, I rehearse, I perform, I go home to my hotel. Some cities are better than others, so are some nights. I thought I was good tonight. I wanted to be. For you."

"You couldn't help being good."

Emma put down her brush and turned to look directly at Deedee. "Still?" she asked bluntly.

It was hard to meet her look, but Deedee did. "Yes. You're an artist, Emma."

Emma smiled wryly. The ear that had helped her change her own speech caught every nuance in someone else's. There was a knock at the door, and she opened it. An assistant stage manager had come for her three Yorkies, dead to the world in their basket in a corner of the dressing room. He often took them to Emma's hotel suite when she was going directly to a party.

Emma picked up a little evening bag. "The artist is ready," she said. "Shall we go?"

It was instantly a party. The caravan of cars and taxis arrived all at once, everybody talking at once, getting into the food, into the drinks, sprawling over the furniture, lolling on the floor. Shoes came off immediately, jackets followed. Deedee turned up the air-conditioning, whisked Emma through a grand tour of the house, darted about on blissfully bare feet. She dug out extra plates and glasses, dipped in and out of conversations, paused only to get vodka refills from Wayne, who was pouring liquor as generously as if his father had been an oilman like Ken Fernbacher's, not a failed, dream-ridden geologist. He'd thrown his jacket over a bookcase, his belly was inching over his belt, but she didn't care. Her house was filled with dancers; her past was part of their present. She belonged to the family.

"*Now* what are you doing?" she asked Emma gaily.

"I hate this picture." Handing her little evening bag and champagne to Michael, Emma turned the picture of herself to the wall. "I'm going to send you a lovely new one. Several. How many bedrooms?"

"You've seen them all. Want to see the cellar? We don't have one." Deedee laughed and went off to make sure Adelaide was being paid court.

Emma took her drink and bag from Michael. "I'm overdressed."

"So am I."

"But subtly," said Peter, who was the company's ballet master and Michael's lover, the former for ten years, the latter for nine. Denmark turns out more than its share of fine male dancers; Peter had been one of the finest until he tore the cartilage in his left knee so badly it had to be removed. Much younger than Michael, he had an ulcer. He was the reason Michael didn't.

Their relationship puzzled Emma because it pleased her. Not as close with Peter as she was with Michael, still she was fond of him, and he respected her. She thought he had a very good sense of humor for a Dane, he thought she had a very good sense of humor for a ballerina. Nobody else thought either was funny at all except Michael who loved them both.

Emilia, sitting on the floor in a corner with Ethan, didn't think Emma was overdressed. Beautiful feet belonged in beautiful shoes; diamond earrings belonged offstage like a diamond tiara belonged onstage; a dress of silk . . .

"She stinks," Ethan said through a mouthful of chicken salad. "You see her fall off that lousy double pirouette? I'll bet Mom would've been a better Anna Karenina."

"You're stupid." Emilia watched Emma move gracefully to Freddie Romoff, who was drinking too much. "Couldn't you see what Emma has?"

"No. What?"

Emilia tried to find the words and failed. She shook her head. "All I know is, I never saw anything like it before."

"And you call me stupid! *There's* what nobody ever saw anything like before!" Ethan pointed a mayonnaised finger at Yuri.

His new idol sat in a big armchair, fondling Willa, the dazzling little Eurasian girl in his lap. Wayne was pouring fresh drinks for them and Michael.

"You know what this fantastic little Russian is going to do, Michael?" he said. "He's going to make it respectable for American boys to be dancers!"

"That won't be entirely due to his dancing," Michael said, and they all laughed.

Watching them, Ethan laughed, too. Not that he got the joke; he just enjoyed seeing everybody laugh.

"You know a secret," Emma said to Wayne.

"Nope. All I know is that she's got something she wants to talk to you about."

Emma felt a little twist of envy; surprising, because twenty years ago she had recognized that Wayne would be good for Deedee. Well, well. She smiled. "You don't have a brother?"

"No. But thank you." He smiled back, and taking her empty champagne glass, made his way to the kitchen. He was getting a new bottle of champagne out of the fridge when

Deedee sailed in, flushed and happy from more than the glass of vodka she carried.

"Oh, beat me to it!"

Wayne worked the cork carefully. "Darn nice of her to have brought it."

"It's all she drinks these days, my dear."

"Chicken. You haven't really talked to her yet, have you?"

"I've been too busy talking to everybody else. Oh, Wayne, I love them all over again! They're family! I wish they'd never leave, or we'd go with them, or . . ." She saw the impossibility in his face and put her head against his chest. "Oh, what the hell." She raised her glass. "Your eyes."

He raised the opened champagne bottle. "Your ass."

She grabbed the bottle and sailed out, laughing.

The patio was pleasantly warm and quiet. The sliding glass doors muffled the noisy voices inside, and the little colored lights, silently twinkling on and off, made the backyard the garden of a villa.

Emma was easier, although, even with her diamond earrings tucked away in her evening bag, she thought she looked wrong, that she was out of place. She hadn't gone to a company party in years; perhaps she should have. The house was small, cramped; yet, unlike her apartment in New York, it was a house people lived in.

Even listening now to Emilia—and it had been an effort to get her to talk—she wondered what it was like to live with other people. She allowed herself to drink more champagne than usual, and enjoyed it.

"But with all that experience," she said to Emilia, "you're really a professional."

"Oh, no."

"Oh, yes. Would you like to take class with the company in the morning?"

To Emma's surprise, she didn't get immediate, blushing acceptance. That intrigued her. The girl's strange blue eyes glinted with a steel she recognized.

"It's pointless to be shy, Emilia," she said brusquely. "You must know what you want, and you must say it."

"I know some things I want."

"Such as?"

Through the glass doors, Emilia saw her father, her first and best teacher, put his arm around her mother. She looked down at Emma's beautiful feet. "To take class with the company," she said with a smile that made her look so much a mischievous little girl that Emma had to laugh.

Absolute children, Janina thought. And dumb. Especially that Carolyn Kingsley. No matter that Emilia had assured her Carolyn had terrific technique and was sure to become a ballerina. Even Janina had recognized that when Carolyn did Black Swan. But that didn't take brains. Carolyn was lucky she was a beauty, and she was; black hair and white skin like Emma's, long legs, tall. Too tall; she was going to have trouble finding the right partner. A pity, because she *was* sweet, but dumb? My God! When Janina'd complimented her on her performance, Carolyn (adjusting her feather boa before Deedee's pier glass—they *all*, male and female, preened endlessly in that glass) had said, "Thank you, Janina. I always try my bestest."

Janina hadn't been able to believe her ears. "Say, Carolyn, where'd you go to school?"

"Well, my first real good teacher was Walter in Chicago; then I took from Maria; but it was really Mme. Dahkarova in New York who—"

"No, Carolyn. I meant where did you learn English?"

"Pardon?"

Pardon! Well, birdbrain Carolyn was having a good time, they were all having a good time, the party was a smash. Janina was very happy for Deedee. And the food was really a smash. Proudly she put on rubber gloves to rinse the dirty dishes and stack them in the machine.

Ethan brought in another stack and dumped them on the butcher-block island, right next to Adelaide, who was perched on a stool, eating as though she was still a dancer. Janina looked at the still-handsome, gaunt old woman and was amazed.

"How do you stay so thin?"

"I never eat," Adelaide said, chewing away.

"I don't understand."

"Nobody understands anything I do, dearie. I don't myself. Had I understood thirty-eight years ago what I was going to be in for, I never would have started this bloody ballet company. I had just one thought: we need a first-class American company."

"You've got a lot of foreigners in yours."

"Dance is international." Adelaide dismissed the criticism airily and gulped her wine. "My company has almost gone under five times, but here we are—the best ballet company in the world."

"Well, in this country, anyway."

Adelaide examined her thoughtfully. "Is that how you were brought up?"

Janina smiled. "Yes."

"Mm. Your mother. Well, I want her and your father to introduce me to some rich oil folk. They have a ballet school, dearie, and that always means half a dozen very lumpy little girls with very rich big daddies. Oh, I won't hurt their business, Janina. I know how to handle the rich. You give them hope, they give you money. Don't put that ham away."

"Save the commercial, Adelaide." Deedee had walked in with a tray of dirty glasses. "Janina doesn't have a penny."

"She should open a restaurant." Adelaide cut herself another slice of ham.

Wayne didn't care how late they stayed or how hungover he would be in the morning. Reminiscing and catching up were fun. Unlike Deedee, he hadn't missed the company; he never looked back; she and the three children were his applause. He always enjoyed others; he was a good friend, perfect for all those who regarded a friend as someone who listened, for he was a wonderful listener. He really looked at you, really listened, really cared. But he didn't need; and sensing that, others found him very attractive, wanted to get through to him, to be special to him. Now, one of the dancers, Arnold Berger, wanted to impress him.

Arnold's vitality was equaled only by his ambition, and both ran second to his determination. His smile was a warning; it switched on and off like a burglar's flashlight. Although he never wasted time on people who were of no use to him either professionally or sexually, here he was wasting time with Wayne. He wanted Wayne to like him, and Wayne, who needed badly to urinate, listened patiently, as though Arnold's need was greater. He leaned against the wall opposite the closed bathroom door and tried to concentrate on Arnold.

"Listen," the boy pushed on, "ballet's no exception. In this country, they want something new every damn minute. So we got to hit 'em with something really original every season."

"I take it you want to become a choreographer," Wayne said politely, offending Arnold.

"I *am* a choreographer!" He realized Wayne had seen him dance and had judged him good, but not good enough. Also too short. He was raging, so he flashed his smile. "I've already done one ballet for Adelaide, and she's hot for me to do another."

"I'm sorry. I didn't know."

"That's all right, fella."

Wayne knew it wasn't. "Living out here ..." he started to explain, but the door to the bathroom opened, and Yuri's Eurasian girl came out. Wayne smiled gratefully and started in, only to bump into Yuri who was coming out, too.

Adelaide, long ready to leave, put her glass down so hard it almost broke. Michael glanced at Peter; Peter picked up Adelaide's crocheted shawl; Arnold went right on, pressing for a commitment for his ballet. He was too new to the upper echelon to know that Adelaide loathed discussing business at parties unless *she* wanted something.

"You might at least tell us a little something about the bloody ballet itself," she snapped.

Arnold tried charm. "It won't have a piano onstage."

"Well," Michael said, "that's a little some-thing."

"But not enough to guarantee you'll do it in the New York season. Don't run, Adelaide."

She took her shawl from Peter. "Arnold, I told you Michael and I would do our best. And I never run." She walked away, calling for Deedee so she could say good night and go home.

Arnold turned to Michael. "How do you get anywhere with her?"

"By realizing she knows exactly what she's doing." He picked up his glass; it was empty, so he took a drink from Peter's. Then, as though he had just thought of it: "By the way, we'd like a new ballet for Emma this season. You don't have to use her, Arnold. It's just a thought."

He turned and followed Peter into the den. They moved quickly out of range of the front door, where Adelaide was saying good night to all five of the hosts. Michael didn't want to take her home. He just wanted to sit and relax and get a little drunk.

Adelaide knew he was ducking her. She didn't blame him. She always got irritable at parties; they were hard work, harder if there was nothing for her to accomplish by going. Still, she was glad she had come; Deedee and Wayne were obviously flattered. Not many were anymore; everybody had a ballet com-pany these days.

"Were you pleased tonight?" she asked Dee-dee. "With Emma?"

"Very."

Adelaide turned to Janina. "I made Emma, dearie."

"No, you didn't," Deedee corrected. "Michael did. You helped."

Adelaide looked pointedly at the glass of vodka in Deedee's hand. "Booze brings out the nitpickers. I might have helped make you, too."

"Really?" Ethan said. "Wow!"

Janina eyed her mother. "Were you as good as Emma?"

"I was different," Deedee said after a moment, aware of Emilia and Wayne in the doorway behind her.

"Very," Adelaide said dryly.

"Different how?" Emilia asked.

Adelaide looked at Deedee and Wayne, then at their elder daughter. "Your mother preferred to get married." She sounded as though she had been betrayed.

In their bedrooms, the children were asleep, even Emilia, who had had a long discussion with Janina over what outfit to wear when she took class with the company. In the living room, Yuri played his guitar woozily and sang in Russian to his girl, who didn't know whether the song was sad or happy, but it was pretty, and he was and he thought she was, so she was happy. On the floor, one's head on the other's chest, two young corps-de-ballet boys listened to Yuri, each wondering why he hadn't realized before that the other was a possible lover. On the couch, a girl slept with her feet in the fifth position.

In the den, three middle-aging, pleasantly half-drunk men—Wayne, Michael, and Peter—listened to a fourth, Freddie Romoff, peacefully bemoaning his life.

"In those days . . ." Freddie's Byronic head slipped off a cushion. He propped himself up again. "In those days, Emma was five pounds lighter and I didn't have this goddamn knee. Michael, why don't you choreograph a new ballet for Emma and me? Something terribly contemporary—like where she lifts me."

"The typewriter's too old," Michael said. "Stiff with arthritis, Freddie. Won't spell out the words."

"Untrue." Peter was sitting on the arm of Michael's chair; he let his hand drop to Michael's shoulder.

"I wish I could quit." Freddie looked at Wayne, drinking beer from a can. "Tell me it isn't the pits to have a ballet school in a cultural toilet."

"It isn't the pits to have a ballet school in a cultural toilet," Wayne said.

"Well, Annabelle wouldn't live in a house like this," Freddie complained. "Annabelle has to have a duplex in New York. Annabelle has to send the *kinder* to private schools. Annabelle has to have sit-down dinner parties. Christ, she was a lousy dancer! Feet like spoons." Michael began to giggle. "True. Pushes me into crappy TV shows for the bread, and then complains all I can talk about is ballet. She gave me a book on Zen . . . I think it was Zen."

"No," Peter said. "Michael and I gave you the book on Zen."

Freddie paid no attention. "And you know what *she* talks about? Money. Bitch. What do you and Deedee talk about, Wayne?"

Wayne grinned. "Money. Ballet."

"We shouldn't've gotten married," Freddie said. "Why did you?"

Was Freddie really asking? He'd been in the company back then: he was at the wedding. So was Michael. He'd been best man. Wayne looked at Michael, who'd always understood.

Michael looked at Freddie. "Why did you?"

Freddie looked at Wayne, then at Michael and Peter. "Why did you?"

They all burst into laughter, which carried cheerfully across the living room and out the now-open doors to the cool patio, where Deedee was stretched out on an old redwood chaise, looking for the moon through the little colored lights. A light breeze stirred the poplars; their leaves looked like silver swaying. The lovely evening was ending, and she would turn back into a pumpkin.

In the corner by the kitchen door, Emma poked at the pile of junk a family with kids manages to collect and never gets around to sorting. She found a fishing rod, held it out awkwardly. Even so, even without the diamond earrings, Emma still looked elegant and chic. She reminded Deedee of the first act of *Giselle*: royalty visiting the schmucky peasants; and taking off those earrings was a small insult.

"Fishing!" Emma exclaimed joyfully. "You didn't actually go fishing!"

Deedee sipped her vodka. "Yeah, and we actually caught fish."

"Oh, take me fishing, Deedee!"

"We don't go anymore. Our school's open all summer. Now, of course"—she waved her hand grandly—"we have it flown in."

Emma put the rod down and came back to the wide redwood chair she had been sitting in. "I'll never go fishing," she said mournfully, taking off her shoes.

"You want to go, you can go." Deedee's tone was pleasant.

"God, dancers have ugly feet!" Emma put hers down on the cool stone. They were beautifully shaped, with a high arch, but the misshapen toes were covered with bunions and calluses. She picked up her champagne. "If I were a man, I could have had all the fish, I mean children I wanted, and still danced."

"How many children?"

"Oh, three." Emma smiled affectionately at Deedee. "Like yours."

"And a husband like Wayne."

"Yes." She looked away, out at the pale garden. "You're a lucky girl."

"Want to change places?" Deedee waited, then shook her head. "Uh-uh. I can't see you teaching a pack of spoiled kids. Or living in a town where the company finally, finally comes—and it's for a Two Night Stand Only. You picked the life you wanted, Emma, me darlin'."

Emma nodded. "So did you."

"Not really," Deedee said softly. "You didn't let me."

"How not?"

"'How not?' Boy, you've picked up some fancy-shmancy expressions along the way up."

"Deedee"—Emma sat up—"I honestly don't have a clue what you're talking about."

"You don't remember when Michael started to choreograph *Anna?*"

"Of course I do!"

"Who was he rehearsing as Anna?"

"You and me."

"And?"

"And ..." Emma struggled to think her way back, to sift out what Deedee was getting at. Ah! "And you got pregnant!"

"And you got nineteen curtain calls."

Emma was startled. "You resent me for *that?*"

Oh, she did sense the resentment. "No. Not for—"

"Do *you* want to change places? I don't get

nineteen curtain calls anymore. Well"—a twist
of a smile—"nobody else does, either. But someone will in something else. And it will not be
me." Her voice went flat. "Remember Dahkarova?"

Deedee nodded. In her bedroom there was a
little shrine of pictures of that legend who had
been American Ballet's prima ballerina when
they joined the company. Dahkarova, their
idol.

"Well, she lives now in an apartment in Carnegie Hall that's as old as she is," Emma said
with a matter-of-fact bleakness. "Splattered
with photographs of herself as Giselle. She
coaches. When she can. She rents rooms. When
she can. She was a great ballerina, Deedee, but
Michael never considered her for Anna for one
minute."

"She was too old."

"Exactly." Emma put on her shoes. "Thank
you."

"But, Emma, that's a fact of life!"

"I have to take class in the morning. That's
another fact of life." She stood and walked into
the house, calling, "Who's going to take me
home?"

Deedee felt as though she had opened the
door to the wrong room. Certainly as though
she had been made to dance to someone else's
tune. She hadn't asked what she'd wanted and
hadn't gotten any answers, not really. What she
remembered, Emma didn't. Or said she didn't.

Had Emma been deliberately evasive, or just too preoccupied with her own ... what? Fear. She *was* scared. Well, she had every right to be: it was a rocky time for her. Oh, it was a rocky time for Deedee, too—she wasn't exactly sure why, maybe she didn't want to know exactly why—but it was somehow worse for Emma. Emma was badly in need.

She caught up with her outside the front door. At the bottom of the little winding walk to the curb, Michael waited by the hired car with Peter.

"I did something wrong, didn't I?" Emma asked.

"What?"

"I wish I knew." It sounded like a joke, and Deedee laughed, but Emma had not meant it as a joke. "Wayne said there was something you wanted to talk to me about."

"I've put it on Hold."

"Tell me."

"I don't remember." She didn't want to upset Emma anymore, she wanted to be close, so she linked arms with her and walked her down the path.

"Perhaps tomorrow ..." Emma began, then stopped walking. "Oh! I almost forgot. I invited Emilia to take class with the company tomorrow."

Deedee lit up. "Oh, Emma!"

"Well! Then I also did something right, didn't I?"

Laughing, Deedee hugged her tightly. "Ohhh
. . . go home!" She kissed Emma, then watched
as she got into the car that would take her back
to her hotel and her three little dogs.

Wayne came out of the house and slipped his
arm around her. "Talk it out with her?"

"Sort of."

A half-assed answer that didn't satisfy him,
and she knew it. The anger at Emma she had
held down now flared up and switched to
Wayne; then, just as quickly, switched to herself. She hadn't known it was inside her, so it
frightened her. And with it came a bitter taste
of somewhere along the way having been
cheated. But she wasn't really sure who had
cheated her, and she knew she had to find out.
Even if she had done it herself.

Chapter Three

Howard, the American Ballet pianist who was alternating between the diaries of Ned Rorem and Anaïs Nin, thumped as loudly as possible in the cavernous pit of the empty old theater. Onstage, in front of the drop from *Anna Karenina*, the company was taking morning class from Peter. More sweat than usual was the only evidence of the Rogers party the night before. Although the outfits were a ragtag grab bag of torn tights and leotards, shirts, half-skirts, plastic and woolen leg warmers, each dancer managed to evolve a dress style as personal as his dance style.

In a far corner far in the wings, Emma finished her own warm-up herself. She was careful, as careful as in her choice of practice clothes which, despite leg warmers, retained her elegance. She put on a long, heavy sweater, wrapped a thick towel around her neck, and moved to the edge of the stage where she watched Emilia with a shrewd, sharp, expert eye.

It was in performance that Emma, like all dancers, had developed and risen to the top rank. But it was in class that she had been discovered and chosen. Like Deedee. They had been doing the customary classroom combinations, but it had taken the ballet master only a few minutes before he moved them to the front row. Watching Emilia now, she was reminded of Deedee's technique and exuberance, but the girl's musical phrasing was her own, as individual as her delicately refined style. Emilia was good; perhaps better than good.

Emma caught Peter's eye. He called for more difficult combinations: one demanding speed, another sustained balance, another lyricism. His eyes traveled from Emilia to Emma; she returned his message of delight and went out front to sit with Adelaide and Michael.

"Good, isn't she?"

"Mmm." From Michael.

Keeping her voice low, she filled them in on Emilia's background, beyond Wayne and Deedee. "She had a scholarship with Carmelita in Los Angeles ... danced with the Houston Ballet, Santa Fe."

"Lots of money in Santa Fe," Adelaide said.

"She's done *Giselle* already."

"Where?"

"Dallas."

"Oh. Dallas." Adelaide sniffed. "The Southwest has such gall."

"What do you think, Michael?" Emma persisted.

He held up his hand, silently telling her to stop pushing. She sat back, trying to relax, watching the judges more than Emilia. She tried to imagine what Deedee would feel, what Wayne would feel if Emilia were asked to join the company. She wondered how she herself would feel, and why she cared.

Patty Mae Davis, the pianist for the Rogers School of Ballet, was sympathetic to Wayne sweating out his hangover as he gave class to a teenage assortment. He was always so considerate of her hangovers, which were chronic. As patient with her as he was with his pupils, some of whom she literally ached to clout on bad days. Not Wayne: he handled them so gently. He was the gentlest man in Oklahoma City. Probably the handsomest, too. For his age, which was ten years more than hers. But he'd had a career and she knew she never would. She liked to pretend she had arthritis in her hands.

In the little office next to the studio, Deedee tried to ignore the throbbing piano and concentrate on the books. She was always behind with the books; she didn't like doing them, but she was very good at them, and Wayne wasn't. She wished he'd give the kids another combination. Every time they jumped, the floor shook; she thought her rattling head would roll off. Perhaps it was the sun sparkling on the glass partition between her desk and the hall that made her think of Emma's diamond earrings. In the shining glass she saw herself on stage as Anna, saw herself in Emma's chair in the dressing room putting on the diamond earrings while Emma watched, saw Emma pick up the photograph of Emma's wedding day. But it had been her wedding, not Emma's, and she thought about why she had gotten married, what she hadn't said to Wayne, what she still hadn't.

The outer door to the shopping mall opened. The explosion of sunlight almost blinded her to the little figure in a baseball suit who ran in and dashed into the boys' dressing room. In a moment she was up and after him. He was frantically stripping off his uniform.

"Women aren't allowed in here!" Ethan bellowed.

"I suppose the game was called on account of rain."

"It wasn't a game, only practice."

"You're going to be kicked off the team."

"No, I won't." Ethan continued to undress.

"Oh, you think you're so valuable!"

"No, but they do. Ha-ha."

"Ethan. Out—and home."

"It's Dad's advanced class, Mom!" he pleaded.

"I know the schedule."

"I'm not gonna miss that class, so you can type your bills and save your breath."

"You save yours, and get this straight! You

want to play baseball? Finish practice. You want to dance? Get to class on time. Personally, I prefer baseball. Athletes last longer and make a helluva lot more money. But either way, follow the rules. Got it?"

She always treated him as an adult, so he always knew when she was right. "Got it," he muttered.

She waited until he had dressed, then watched him trudge off across the hot, sunlit mall. When he got to the red dirt at the edge of the road, he kicked it hard. He wasn't her son for nothing.

She turned to go in, then saw the pickup truck parked beyond the Cadillacs in front of the plant nursery and the water-bed shop. She was certain Mr. Fleetwood would be leaning against the front fender, waiting. She walked over, folding her arms as she did. He remained completely impassive, just a big middle-aged American Indian in neat western clothes leaning against his old truck. She had been through this before. She waited.

"Too hot for you out here," he said finally.

She continued to wait.

"I told you, I ain't payin' for any lessons, Mrs. Rogers."

Today she could outwait him; today she could get him to move.

"Throw the kid out of your school," he suggested.

"Oh, you'd like that?"

"Do us all a favor."

"Really?" Suddenly furious, she couldn't wait. "Mr. Fleetwood, excuse me, but you're a schmuck. You afraid your kid's going to be a sissy? You think my kid is? My husband was a dancer."

"So I heard."

She had set it up, she wanted that fuel. "Yeah? You know, I'm goddamn sick of you insulting my husband and my kid and your kid with your incredible schmuckiness. Your kid is better than any athlete in this cornball, bigoted town! If you don't care a hoot in hell about him, why do you always come to pick him up? Now you get in there and watch him for once!"

But Fleetwood just stood, aware that she was somehow as angry at herself as she was at him. She knew it too, and started back to the school. But the kid was more important than her anger or his father's stubbornness or her pride. She came back and begged softly: "Ah, come on, Mr. Fleetwood. The kid's been waiting for you for months."

Like a mother, she took his hand, and he followed her into the classroom where they stood by the door, clearly separate from the mothers sitting on a bench against the wall. The kids were facing the mirror and Wayne. She saw Wayne's eyes flicker over Mr. Fleetwood, then heard him call a flashy combination.

Like his father, the Fleetwood kid showed no

reaction. His hard-muscled, arrowlike little brown body cut through the air without missing a beat. His turns were fast, precise; he had more elevation than anyone in the class; he was unafraid. If he was a little too athletic, a layman wouldn't have known. He ended the combination cleanly, exactly with the music, and stood sweating, breathing hard, looking at his position in the mirror. Then Wayne deliberately moved and in the mirror, the boy saw his father standing by the door, watching. His big face as impassive as ever, he was trying to smile. He tried hard, but he couldn't somehow, so he just nodded. Again and again and again as his kid's generous mouth opened in a smile big enough for both of them.

"If she's not here by a quarter past, we're eating," Ethan announced.

He and Wayne were setting the round dining table; Deedee, her hair again in curlers, stood at the butcher block, mixing a salad; Janina was seasoning a lamb stew she had made in the pressure cooker after school. The late-afternoon sun reddening their faces cast a calm, lazy glow over the tenseness in the kitchen; but outside, the hot wind shook the poplars, bounced the strings of colored bulbs, stirred up every plant in the yard. More like it, Deedee thought.

"This need more of anything?" Janina held out a spoonful of gravy.

"Uh-uh. Delicious." She picked up her martini and turned to Wayne. He lifted his glass—to make a silent toast, she thought—but he merely took a swallow. She couldn't decide what he was hoping for Emilia, whether he feared losing her.

"Dad," Ethan said, "is it true Yuri does doubles in the air and then a twist and then comes down on one knee?"

"So I hear."

"Jesus!"

"My girlfriends couldn't care if he did triples and came down in a split," Janina said. "They just want to see him in tights."

"And you don't!" Ethan challenged.

Janina stirred the stew. "Dancers are boring. They're all in love with themselves. It's those mirrors."

"Dad, did you hear what Janina said?"

"Daddy and Mama are teachers, not dancers. And you're neither."

"Is that so?" Ethan said angrily.

"As a matter of fact, yes."

"Mom . . ."

"Oh, Ethan, if you don't know by this time when she's kidding . . ." Deedee broke off as the back door opened and Emilia came in, carrying her practice bag. They stared, waiting; her eyes were unreadable.

"O.K.!" Ethan blurted out impatiently. "What?"

"They asked me to join the company," Emilia said quietly.

"I knew it!" Ethan shouted, and they ran to hug her, all of them shouting at once, all except Deedee.

She was suddenly old. She was in her early forties, but she was old. A lifetime had passed since she joined the company; she'd had her chance; it was gone, it was over; her place was taken. She was old.

"All right, quiet down, everybody," she said brusquely. She kissed Emilia. "When do you start?"

"With rehearsals in New York. Before their summer season there." She didn't seem very excited.

"What's the matter, honey?" Wayne asked.

She clung to him. "I didn't tell them I'd go, Daddy."

"Jerk!" Ethan said.

"Ethan!"

"I said I wanted to think it over."

"Why, for God's sake?" Ethan sat down disgustedly.

Janina gave him a poke. "Because she's got more brains than you have, you little creep! She knows it's the fork in her road."

Deedee laughed. "The what??"

"Well, it is," Emilia said seriously. "And I want to know where I'm going."

"Right. Why shouldn't you?" Wayne pulled Emilia closer, looking at Deedee over her head.

"Yes, it's very smart of you, Emilia," Deedee said. "Now come on. Let's eat or we'll be late for the performance."

Janina was relieved when Emma said she had to pack; the company was leaving practically at dawn. Nice as she was, Emma was oddly unsettling to her mother; it was good that they got their good-byes over in Emma's dressing room. Besides, she didn't think she could take another night of continuous yammering about ballet.

When she was little, she'd taken class as Emilia had. But when dancing lessons began cutting into her extracurricular activities at school and her new friendships, Janina announced she was quitting. Neither Wayne nor Deedee objected. They were mystified that she really liked school, more mystified by her high grades, but delighted that, unlike Emilia, she had so many good friends. The telephone rang for Emilia, but Emilia didn't seem to care. As with Wayne, the family and ballet were enough. Janina was her closest friend. Sometimes Deedee thought she had gotten their ages confused and that Janina was the elder. And sometimes Janina thought she was older than all of them, including her mother and father.

When they got home and were undressing in their bedroom, Janina asked, "Decided about joining the company?"

Emilia shook her head.

Janina sighed: it was going to be another late night.

Deedee saw the crack of light under their door and was glad they were so close. She didn't want to influence Emilia one way or the other, nor did she want Wayne to. She got two cans of beer from the fridge and went into the den where Wayne sprawled in his armchair. He made a face.

"Beer?"

"We've both been drinking too much."

"Deedee, last night—"

"Was an excuse, not an exception." She flopped into her chair. "The air-conditioner in the office is still on the fritz."

"They said they'd get at it first thing in the morning."

"They always say that, but they never say what morning. Why do you think she's hesitating about joining the company?"

"She probably won't admit it, but she feels funny about leaving us."

"So do I. Even funnier. I get a picture of Janina going off to college. Then Ethan . . ." She rubbed her face against the cold beer can. "Emma travels with three little dogs."

"Would you rather Emilia didn't join?"

"Oh, God, no. I don't want her to spend her life buried in Oklahoma City."

Wayne took off his shoes so that she couldn't see his face. "If she does go, you ought to think of going to New York for the summer."

"You always baby her," Deedee said, pretending to misunderstand.

"She doesn't make friends as easily as Janina does."

"She will in the company."

"There's always a lot of jealousy in the company."

"Well, that never bothered you, so why don't you go? Why should I go?"

He laughed. "Stop bullshitting. You know you want to go, you know we've got to keep the school open, and you know I'm a better teacher than you are."

"Only in the summer. It's too damn hot here for me."

"So go to New York."

"Where it's cool?" She grinned, but her heart was pounding. "Anyway, I can't leave the other kids."

"Janina's happy as a clam here, and Ethan—"

"I know: he'd kill to study there. Plus the ball games."

"So?"

"Oh, Jesus." Anything and everything drew tears these days. "You know me so damn well. I do want to go to New York."

"I think you have to."

"Oh, trying to get rid of me?" she joked.

"No. Trying to hold on to you."

Opening night, but neither would raise the curtain for fear the past would make an entrance. They had never before come this close to playing out the scene. Each unaware it was the same scene, they sat silently, finishing their beer, pretending they weren't quivering inside—Deedee because her fantasies of New York flooded her with guilt, Wayne because he knew he not only was taking the risk of losing her but also the risk of losing himself.

Emilia came into the den in her bathrobe.

"I couldn't sleep," she said, "and I figured nobody could until I settled it."

"Which way?" Deedee asked.

Emilia shrugged. "Well ... I'd like to ask two questions."

"Shoot," Wayne said.

"Ethan says I'm scared of competition. I'm not. But it's a really big company, so ... how much will I get to dance?"

"That depends on how good you are, honey," he said.

"Well ... how good am I?"

"Very." He kissed her. "Now, what's the other question?"

"Should I know now whether I want to stay in the company?" She looked from one to the other, revealing nothing. "I mean it seems if you stay, there are things you have to give up."

And vice versa, Deedee wanted to retort. She kept her eyes on the can of beer she was toying with: she was too easy for both of them to read. And here was one of those times when she wasn't sure how to read Emilia. Maybe she was thinking of Emma; then did she mean she didn't want to be like Emma, or was she afraid of disappointing her parents—well, Wayne anyway—by saying she preferred to be like Emma? Lucky that Deedee was the mother; if she were Wayne, she'd be sure to be speculating whether this changeling wasn't really someone else's.

Not Wayne. He put his arms around his daughter with untroubled affection. "You nut! Deal with whether you stay or not if and when they ask you. For now, just know what you want and do it."

"You sound like Emma, Daddy."

Now Deedee did look at her. "It isn't all that easy to know what you want."

"Oh, for me it is," Emilia said firmly. "I mean I know what I want for now."

"What?"

"Just to dance."

"Then go ahead!" Wayne swooped her up in the air as though he were partnering her.

With delight equal to his, she looked down at her father's handsome face; straightened her back and extended her arms gracefully, as he, her first teacher, had taught her; remembered the first thrilling time he, prince and partner, had guided her through a pas de deux.

It was in the studio after classes. They had a full orchestra on the record player, she wore a tiara she'd made herself, and as they danced, an almost painful rush of joy shot through her. Since then, whenever she danced, even in classroom exercises, she waited for that surge of joy, and, more often than not, it came. With American Ballet, one of the really great companies, rehearsing in New York, dancing at the State Theater in Lincoln Center—surely that joy would be almost constant, practically unbearable! She raised her head and smiled like the ballerinas in the pictures on the walls.

Of course, Emilia was wrong, as she found as soon as she began rehearsals in New York. And Deedee, arriving with her and a suitcase of foolish expectations, quickly found that she, too, was wrong: she hadn't come home, there was no brass band. Familiar faces had disappeared like familiar landmarks. She was an outsider, a visitor in a very busy city, and no one was coming around the corner. Only Ethan, to whom the trip was like going to the moon, couldn't wait to get up every morning and explore the craters.

Emilia could hardly get out of bed. Her constant state was exhaustion. The company rehearsed endlessly, and yet no one ballet was rehearsed often enough. The schedule was a masterpiece of disorganization. All the choreographers and their proxies fought for more time and all lost. A two-minute section of an old ballet would be gone over and over and over; the whole was never polished completely. New ballets were half-finished, roughly outlined, left dangling: stories without endings, unfinished love affairs, patterns made of smoke.

She ran from one rehearsal hall to another, her only guide the bulletin board, never totally sure of what she was doing when, never able just to relax and dance, never able to feel joy. And always, every day, classes, often given by Peter, who had a sharp tongue. He seemed to get real pleasure from being needlessly demanding of her.

In the halls, she ran into Emma who assured her that once the season got under way, there would be more time. But Emma looked as though she had problems of her own, and there were whispers about her that Emilia didn't want to hear.

For years, her mother had talked so glowingly of New York, had made it sound such a magical city. Maybe it was; she wouldn't know. All she saw was a triangle bounded by Lincoln Center, the American Ballet School in the West Sixties, and their apartment on Seventh Avenue; and she was too tired to see even that small area clearly.

They were renting two rooms—one for Emilia and Deedee, one for Ethan—from Mme. Dahkarova, in the Carnegie Hall building. They had the run of the big, musty apartment, except for the double-doored living room which Dahkarova used as a studio for her coaching. The large room across the hall—there was a kitchen in an alcove that Deedee found adequate—was used for living room, dining room, all-purpose room. Like the other rooms, like the rooms back home in Oklahoma, its walls were splashed with ballet photographs. Except that these were mainly of Dahkarova during her triumphant career. And Russian icons and paintings of Russian saints kept reminding you of her origins, even in the bathrooms.

Like Dahkarova, the apartment and everything in it were old, faded and yet exciting. At least, it would have been exciting if Emilia weren't so dulled by exhaustion and confusion. It was all strange: being in a ballet company, being away from home, living without her father, sharing a room with her mother instead of her sister. She was aware that Deedee was disappointed in something. Maybe that she'd only had two brief lunches with Emma—no, Emilia sensed it was more than that. Every evening, with a desperation Emilia had never seen before, Deedee would ask endless questions about the day, about Emma, about Michael, about this one and that one. Emilia fell asleep even as she was dredging up answers. Still, Deedee insisted on washing out her tights for her, massaging Bengué into her sore muscles, chattering all the time about her determination to get a summer scholarship for Ethan and a teaching job for herself, both at the company's school. But she kept saying it, and nothing happened. And when the phone rang, it was either for Mme. Dahkarova or Wayne or Janina were calling from Oklahoma.

Although Emilia had studied for so many years that twisting her body into distorted, unnatural positions was as natural to her as to ballet, and although she had appeared in the Southwest with professional companies, she had never thought of dancing as painful, punishing, grueling *work*. That, she understood now, was because she had never been in a major international company, had never gone through the lunatic crash-course preparations for a big New York season. She wondered why neither Wayne nor Deedee had ever talked about that side of ballet, whether it was why they had given up dancing so early.

Until one airy summer morning when she found herself strolling up Broadway to American Ballet's school. *Strolling*, not hurrying, not dragging, strolling. Her stomach was peaceful, the warm sun felt lovely, her clean hair felt lovely, the trees were green, her legs didn't ache, and her feet hardly hurt. Sweat and pain had at last become as routine as the drive for a perfect arabesque. She looked forward to class with Peter, to all the rehearsals. And that day, Peter kissed her after class, and Michael gave her a small part—one of the Three Girls in Blue—in the first cast of one of the opening-night ballets.

When she brought home the news that evening, she was disappointed Ethan wasn't there: he was having supper at the house of a kid he played ball with in the park. But Mme.

Dahkarova got as excited as he would have and Deedee, who had limped through another hot day trying to corner Adelaide about her job, burst into tears and called Wayne. He wasn't home, which stabbed her, until she remembered they were on different time.

Emilia was pleased, not excited. Her joy was in her own dancing, not in performing for others. Without that joy, dancing, even in this superior company, was merely hard work. If she left, her father would be disappointed. He wouldn't say so, of course, but he would be, and she didn't think she could bear that.

Opening night, the company reached a pitch of excitement equaled by its nervousness. One goes with the other; Emilia had little of either. Made-up and dressed early, she stood calmly in the wings watching with surprise as the under-rehearsed ballets came together. She studied the different brilliance of Emma and Sevilla, the precision of the corps, the assured swiftness of the soloists.

Onstage, they were all beautiful, all effortless and serene, all royal inhabitants of an airy kingdom. No reality to threaten the audience; only noble gossamer that it could identify with in its dreams. Onstage, dancers *were* dream creatures; offstage, they sweated and gasped, aching athletes in the locker room of the wings. As Emilia watched, they came flying off with charmed smiles, then grabbed Kleenex from the boxes attached to the light stands to blot their soaking bodies, grunting as though they had been on the rack. One or two inhaled oxygen; another ran to the nearest toilet to throw up; another fell to the floor in pain from a torn tendon—and went back on. Sandra, the nonstop talker and giggler from Puerto Rico who dressed next to Emilia, came spinning off to loud applause. She burst into tears anyway. "I can't turn for shit tonight," she cried. Emilia, now about to make her debut with American Ballet on the stage of the State Theater in Lincoln Center, New York City, patted Sandra's eyes with Kleenex, hugged her, and got into position for her first entrance.

With her first *grand jeté*, her mind ceased being a governor. The surge of music from the huge orchestra was matched by the surge of joy she had thought would never come again. Joy lifted her high in the air, whirled her in a circle of perfect piquet turns, parted her lips in a smile she didn't know was there. It was, after all, worth all the work.

She beamed all through the curtain calls, standing in a line with the other soloists, the corps de ballet behind them, as bouquet after bouquet was brought out for Carolyn, who had danced the leading role with Yuri as her partner. She watched Carolyn pluck a previously loosened rose from a bouquet and hand it to Yuri, and heard the audience cheer. She looked out at the huge crowd in the sparkling auditorium, saw fans run down the aisles with more flowers, saw the heavy gold curtain swing down and Carolyn and Yuri run out in front for their own bows—gracious royalty from an unattainable realm. When they came back behind the curtain between bows, Emilia saw that their makeup was running, their bodies were gushing sweat; they were gasping and limping, but their elation was like a glorious halo.

She realized, then, that there was another kind of joy from dancing. And wondered what it felt like.

Chapter Four

"O.K. Good-bye," Ethan said impatiently when they reached Broadway and Sixty-third, but Deedee turned the corner with him.

"Now you behave," she lectured. "Remember you're on a scholarship and be grateful."

"Oh, I am. It keeps me off the streets."

"You'd better not be smart-ass with your teachers. They're not your mother."

They arrived at the door with the letters AMERICAN BALLET sparkling in the sun. He switched his little practice bag to give her a firmly final handshake. "Here's where you get off. Good-bye."

He was halfway up the stairs when he heard her behind him. "No!"

She continued to climb. "You won't be seen with me."

"Don't you have anything better to do?" He spat the words out between clenched teeth.

"Frankly, no!" she snapped back.

"Jesus." Ethan shook his head in disgust,

then sighed sympathetically. "Well, let me go first."

She waited until he disappeared, then climbed the rest of the way slowly. The line of mothers sitting on the bench in the reception area turned to her like Rockettes. The one nearest, in her plump thirties, sewing ribbons on a toe shoe, smiled a welcome and inched over to leave a space. Deedee smiled frostily and walked to the young woman at the reception desk as though they were old pals.

"Hello, Florence. Adelaide around by any chance?"

"I'm sorry, but she's at a fund-raising meeting, Mrs. Rogers."

Deedee lowered her voice. "Deedee."

"Deedee." Florence measured out the two syllables.

"Thanks. See you, Florence!" She turned as though she had a destination and saw that a door to one of the rehearsal studios was open. Humming the music along with the piano, she caught a glimpse of herself in the mirrored wall just before one of the dancers closed the door. Still humming, she sauntered past the knowing eyes of the mothers who looked no different than they did in Oklahoma City. No better, either. The entrance door opened for Sevilla, in a long see-through summer dress.

"Sevilla! Hello!"

Sevilla stopped puffing on her cigarette holder and tried to put Deedee in focus. A fan or another mother? "Oh, hello there." That covered everything in America.

Deedee pushed open the door and fled down the stairs, blushing.

On Broadway, it was as hot as Oklahoma City but less soggy. She was conscious of trickles down her back as she walked slowly to Lincoln Center, past the open but breezeless plaza, past the posters in front of the State Theater: AMERICAN BALLET—NOW THRU SEPT. 4.

Inside the stage entrance, it was cool. She asked for Adelaide—what the hell; then for Michael. Two pale young dancers came in from the sun and ambled down the corridor to the elevator with that ducklike walk. She still walked like that herself. She should have waddled right to the elevator without asking for anyone. She wiped her face with her damp handkerchief. The security officer at the front desk was taking his time.

"He's in rehearsal," he said finally. Her futile visits had begun to depress him. "Anyone else?" Then, annoyed that she depressed him: "I got nothing better to do."

"That makes two of us. Want to have a drink?" She clumped out into the heat and stood at the top of the stairs leading down to the stage entrance, trying to decide how to fill the rest of the afternoon.

All her life, she had worked and still accomplished the jobs of housewife and mother quickly and well with Wayne's help and, later,

Janina's. She didn't know how to meet the girls for dawdling lunches and shopping any more than she knew how to drag out household chores. Her part of Dahkarova's apartment was cleaned, the laundry done, the marketing done, supper could be on the table within thirty minutes after Emilia got home. All right, now what? Go to a museum or a gallery or a movie. She had bitched enough about the lack of museums in Oklahoma City, but the truth was she wasn't that mad about museums. And she hated going to the movies alone. She hated going anywhere alone; she'd never had to before. She needed people; they were what she had come to New York for. But everyone she knew in New York was busy. Everybody in New York was busy.

Michael was busy at rehearsal, but the rehearsal wasn't his. A small group of dancers, including Emilia, was sweating through Arnold's new work-in-progress. The ballet was odd, original, perhaps too determined to be contemporary and new. But Arnold was new and young, and, no different from his contemporaries, determined to be different.

He sat watching his dancers like a ravenous storm trooper, his body rigid with tension, his tight lips silently counting for them. Michael understood the tension; but it made dancers tight and nervous, so he never let it show during rehearsals of ballets he created. Used to create.

She smiled wryly at Peter who knew what he was thinking and touched him lightly for an instant. It helped. Michael turned his head to see if there was any reaction so far from Emma: the ballet, after all, was being shown for her benefit. Her approval, really.

In a pale beige leotard and chiffon skirt, she leaned against the *barre*, deceptively still, totally concentrated on Emilia who was merely standing in, demonstrating the role Arnold had worked out on her, presumably for Emma. The girl was so blatantly young, she made Michael uneasy. Arnold was a shrewd cookie who never did anything accidentally. Was he demonstrating to Michael that Emma was too old for the ballet? That it was good enough to be done without her, that it didn't need her?

Arnold clapped his hands sharply: Napoleon commanding his troops to halt. "That's as far as I got," he said.

"Interesting." Emma made the word ambiguous. "Thank you, Emilia." The warmth of her voice was even stronger by contrast.

The room was unnaturally quiet. Howard, who had played the piano at Emma's rehearsals for fifteen years, pressed his wet hands hard against his thighs. The dripping dancers were uncomfortable, embarrassed. Like Emilia, they were all a generation younger than Emma; and the role meant for her, though central to the ballet, wasn't all that big. Not yet, at any rate.

Peter lit a cigarette; Michael took it away and smoked it himself. Emilia, who had thought she was standing in for Carolyn or someone of even less importance in the company, now discovered an emotion new to her: anger. Cold anger at Arnold because of Emma.

"Shall I show you your solo?" he asked Emma.

"Please do." She hung her sweater over the *barre* and followed him out on the floor, where she marked the combinations as he called them. Twice she executed a movement full out, a movement that suited her perfectly, which she could use to show that she was still Emma. There weren't many.

"*Passé, chassé, saut de basque.*" When the combination was familiar, there was relief in Arnold's voice. He flashed his smile encouragingly.

"And a double pirouette." 'As usual,' Emma's tone implied.

"You can do a single." Too gracious.

"I can do a double," she shot back.

And will if it kills you, Michael thought. But he tensed as Arnold's counts became unusually irregular, the movements wrenchingly angular.

"Left arm straight out and hold two counts."

"Where do you want my head?"

"Down and to the side."

Emma knew he meant for her to turn her

head to the right. She turned it down and to the left: she was staring directly into her armpit. "Fascinating," she murmured, and faced him. "It might help, Arnold, if you tell me what I'm supposed to be playing."

"There's no story, Emma, it's abstract." He tried not to sound impatient or superior, but failed.

"I'm aware of that, Arnold. I didn't ask *who* I was playing, I asked *what* I was playing." Her voice suddenly rose. "What am I *feeling?*"

"Nothing," he said icily. "You just dance."

Just dance. She'd been a ballerina longer than he'd been a dancer, longer than any of these children she couldn't look at. She'd not only continued tradition, she'd expanded it, started a new one. She was in all the books. "Arnold," she said evenly, "you got the wrong lady."

She snatched up her sweater and walked out rapidly, Michael only a step behind her.

The dancers were too young to feel they had seen their own futures—if they had the talent to last. All they had seen was the inevitable humiliation of an aging woman in a world for the young. Still, Emma was a ballerina, a star they respected and liked. Nobody moved.

Then Arnold said, "Peter, would you go over what I just did?"

Peter looked at him innocently. "You mean the ballet?"

Arnold left without bothering to answer. He

found Michael halfway down the corridor outside the rehearsal studio talking quietly to Emma who was staring blindly out the big window that framed the city. Rapidly Arnold computerized the battle: Emma and Michael, old friends. Michael the artistic director, Adelaide listens to him. But they need new ballets, new choreographers, him. Did they need Emma? Did he? Yes and no. She was still a star; she could help some, she might hurt more if she wanted more. His own indecision angered him. He was uncertain which way to play it, so he took the offensive. Michael cut him short.

"Watch your blood pressure, Arnold. I did not say that unless you used Emma, we wouldn't put on your ballet. I did say that with Emma, it would get the serious attention it deserves. Actually, that's why you showed it to her, isn't it?"

"I was surprised she was willing to consider being in it."

"Why? You're a young choreographer, Emma has always—"

"Michael." Emma turned sharply from the window. "I am in bad need of a new ballet, Arnold, and you know it. We're using each other. But play fair. You're very talented. Talented enough to change it to what I can do best— *now*."

"I'd like to, Emma, but it's not that simple."

"Little Arnold's ambivalence is showing," Michael said.

"Don't get bitchy, Michael," Arnold snapped.

"I wasn't referring to your sex life, dear."

"Good ballets are for dancers, not to oblige stars."

"I'm afraid he wants his choreography to be the only star," Michael said a little nastily because he understood.

"It is, and it should be. And you, of all people, know it!"

But you have time, Arnold, Michael thought, and my friend Emma's is running out. Like mine.

Emma looked squarely at Arnold. "Then you don't want me."

He was afraid to say it, she could see that. Afraid Michael would cancel the ballet unless he used her. But he had never intended to use her; he knew she couldn't dance that choreography anymore. He'd been teasing them, playing them to get his ballet on the schedule. Oh, maybe he'd hoped that somehow it would work out, somehow she'd be able to do it. But she was as wrong for the ballet as it was for her. Unless he was willing to change it.

His eyes told her he wasn't, that he came first. She couldn't blame him, really. It takes one to know one. "Well, then it *is* that simple." She smiled. "Your choreography looked very good on Emilia. Use her, Arnold. She'll surprise you."

The moment Arnold went back into the rehearsal hall, Emma started to hiccup. Michael put his arm around her and led her down the corridor to the water fountain.

"The little turd didn't even have the grace to talk me into staying in his bloody ballet," Emma said, and hiccupped.

"Drink slowly." Michael handed her the paper cup he'd filled. "By the way, you and Freddie aren't doing any *Giselles* this season."

Emma laughed. "Are you trying to scare the hiccups out of me?"

"No," he said. "Sevilla is doing the first two, then she alternates with—"

"Carolyn." She hiccupped again. He refilled the cup for her. "You chose a lovely time to tell me, Michael."

"It's easier to get everything dumped on you at once."

"Easier for whom?" she asked angrily.

"I'm the artistic director, Emma. You tell me"—he had to stop for a second—"you tell me how and when you would say it to an artist you respect. And a friend you love."

Loving friend: the Chippendale mirror reflecting his bed in the Greenwich Village walk-up; breakfasting in evening clothes in a grubby White Tower diner at glorious dawn after the opening night of *Anna;* holding regretful hands while Deedee and Wayne were being married at City Hall; trying to show only pleasure when he told her about Peter; taking her to supper on her fortieth birthday and never mentioning it; not letting her be alone for one moment until she got the doctor's report that the lump in her breast was only a cyst.

To say what he had just said had been agony for him. He hadn't shown it, any more than she had shown the depths of her own agony. They were each like that; they always had been. Perhaps that was why they remained friends; perhaps why they had never really been lovers.

She took his arm and he took her hand, and they walked slowly to the elevator. He pressed the button for the stage level, where her dressing room was.

"Poor Freddie," Emma said, thinking of his bad knee, of Annabelle and her duplex and her parties. "You know, we're only getting paid by the performance this season."

"No. I didn't know." Damn Adelaide.

The elevator doors slid open. "Well," Emma said brightly, "the hiccups are gone, too."

Emma walked slowly up the steps from the stage entrance. Usually she ran up the steps; usually her schedule was too tight. Today she'd expected to cram in rehearsal for Arnold's ballet, rehearsal for *Giselle*, a fitting for a new first-act costume for *Giselle*. She hadn't had to fill time for twenty years. Even her holiday hours were measured out.

She stared downtown. The hot streets were almost as empty as she was, as her day was.

She turned uptown, walked slowly that way because there were some trees, a few people. On the stone ledge leading up to the plaza, a woman was sitting too listlessly to be sunbathing, to be doing anything. Like the old people and failures sitting in the shade of the trees on the concrete island where the streets converged.

The woman turned in Emma's direction, and at the same moment they called out:

"Deedee!"

"Oh, Emma!"

Gratefully they embraced, endearing words spilling into nervous laughter, and hanging on to each other, headed uptown, then downtown, then, really laughing, almost danced into the wide street to hail a taxi.

They dumped their Bloomingdale's parcels on a settee under one of the photographs of Dahkarova as Giselle.

"Now to find something to stick the posies in," Deedee said.

Emma examined the photograph. "She used to have some really beautiful old cut-glass vases."

"Everything she has now is either a samovar or broken."

Emma left the photograph and started prowling. "What's this mean?" She was frowning at the little blackboard over the telephone stand.

In wavering chalk letters it said: "D-D, Vagne fone."

"Oh, that was last night. You have to break Dahkarova's code."

"Oh . . . Oh! Wayne phoned."

"Give the little lady a big cigar."

"How is he?"

"Fine." And smart, Deedee thought. So smart he knew if he gave her enough rope, she'd hang herself.

"And Janina?"

"Same: crazy. She likes Oklahoma and doesn't like ballet. How did I end up with a normal child?" Small talk, but all talk was easy now. Except talk related to that picture of Emma and herself rehearsing in the mirror. That kind of talk now would break the warm spell, spoil the reunion.

When they came into the apartment, music from a phonograph behind the double doors to Dahkarova's studio had been indistinct, stopped, then, a moment ago, started again. Emma stopped watching Deedee rummage in cabinets and listened: the music was from *Giselle*.

"Ah, you can pass for a vase, me darlin'." Deedee fished out a chipped porcelain pitcher from a cupboard under the sink and began putting the flowers in. "If I could only get that damn teaching job." She picked up the subject left in the elevator on the way up. "All I need is

Adelaide's O.K., but I can't even get the old bitch on the phone."

Emma had moved close to the double doors. "Who's she coaching?"

"What? Oh that tall number's been coming all week. Carolyn?"

"Yes." Emma moved back into the room, sat at the ornate dining table. "I heard Carolyn would be doing *Giselle* this season."

Her carefully composed face said it all; explained the happy day, and soured it. Deedee had thought it was pure friendship that had returned to them the enjoyment of sharing a day. She had felt so close, so equal, that she had felt young. But she should have known by now that Emma couldn't feel pure anything for anyone. Oh, there was friendship, all right, but there was a heavy dosage of desperation, which Emma had hidden from her. For a moment, Deedee felt tricked; then, because she understood Emma's unspoken despair, guilty for feeling tricked; then compassion tainted with perverse pleasure. Then Emma hiccupped as she always did when she was frightened, and Deedee loved her all the more.

"Dammit," Emma said. "Not again."

Deedee hastily got a glass, brought water. "How about if I kill Adelaide. I'd like to anyway."

"Don't blame Adelaide." Slowly Emma drank the water, drowning the hiccups. Her voice was even. "I swore I'd retire at thirty-five. Then thirty-six, thirty-seven, thirty-eight. Then I shut my eyes. How old were you when you began lessons?"

"Eight."

"I wasn't seven. Those weird positions. Our bodies always objected."

"I remember."

"Ah, but you didn't stay long enough to know they revolt. And too soon. They refuse to do what one wants. Well, they can't." She rubbed the table with one finger. "But even now, there are moments when it all comes together—the dancing and the music and the lights and the costumes—it's better than making love." She took a deep breath. "You wanted to know what it's like to be me now. Deedee, all I am doing offstage is waiting to get back on."

For a moment, Deedee wanted to hug Emma tightly, like one of her children. But she knew Emma would take that as pity.

"How about a beer?" she asked. "No. Tea!"

"I'll make it."

"You'll sit on your sitter."

"I'm going to talk to Adelaide about your job."

"You're not going to ask her for a damn thing."

"Not for me, no. I won't mention *Giselle*. And Adelaide will be so relieved, she'll give you the job.

When the kettle was on and the Earl Grey in the pot, Deedee said, "Why do the problems of people like you seem so much more important than the problems of people like me?" She shook her head and grinned. "Obvious. You're more important."

"If I am," Emma said slowly, "it's not for long. A few years ago, Dahkarova coached me. Today, Carolyn. Next year, Emilia."

Deedee paused as she was getting out the teacups. "Emilia?"

"Oh, yes."

"She's that good?"

"She's going to do it *for* you, Deedee."

Deedee turned quickly to the teacups, hiding her face. She was jealous. Proud, yes, but jealous of her own daughter. She couldn't be, shouldn't be, she wasn't. Anyway, if Emilia got there, it would be for Emilia, not for Deedee. Nobody could get there for Deedee now.

The music had stopped a few minutes earlier. Now the double doors were pushed back, and Carolyn came out. In practice clothes, sweaty, but lovely, and young.

"Could I have ... ?" she began in her flat, little-girl voice, then saw Emma. "Oh." She giggled in embarrassment. "Emma. You're here."

"Still," Emma said.

The kettle was whistling. Deedee turned off the gas. "What'd you want, Carolyn?"

"A glass of water?"

Dahkarova had heard the kettle and gaily made her entrance. Her small body was lumpy, her face a crumpled remnant, but her legs and hands were still beautiful.

"Ah, kettle is on!" she said greedily. Although she'd been in the country for thirty years, her accent only seemed to get thicker. Her bright, buried eyes saw Emma.

"*Je regrette.*" The old lady used French to be tactful, but being a survivor herself, she was brusque.

"*Pourquoi?*" Emma shrugged. "*Ce n'est pas ta faute.*"

"*Oui, mais je comprends aussi.*"

"*Je sais. Merci.*" Emma kissed Dahkarova on both cheeks and turned to Carolyn. "*Tu veux du thé?*" She hadn't been able to resist, and was gratified by Carolyn's gaping mouth. "Tea, Carolyn?"

"Oh, I—"

"Sit," Dahkarova commanded. "You have little cake, Deedee?"

"Sure. Anyone else?" She got out more teacups.

"Of course not!" Dahkarova said sharply. "Carolyn has strong technique, Emma. Like us. But here"—she tapped her forehead—"weak. However, nice girl. Correct, Carolyn?"

"Oh, correct," Carolyn agreed.

"You see?" Dahkarova said to Emma, and sat at the table next to her.

The front door slammed, and Emilia came down the hall.

"How'd rehearsal go?" Deedee asked eagerly. Emilia gave her a quick kiss and ran to Emma.

"You won't believe how mean Arnold was after you walked out!"

"It doesn't matter. He's going to give you the part."

"I knew it was your idea!"

"What part?" Deedee asked, but Emilia chattered away excitedly with Emma. "Tea, Emilia?" Deedee cut in sharply.

"Yes, please."

"You'll get the part," Emma said.

Carolyn perked up. "What part?"

"In Arnold's new ballet."

"Who Arnold?" Dahkarova demanded. "Is good ballet?"

"It's a good part for Emilia," Emma said.

"Well, then," Dahkarova said, laying down her eternal law, "you must help and coach her."

Once, Emma had had a Yorkie that survived blindness and tumors and then got pneumonia. Too old, the vet pronounced, finished. Nevertheless, Emma fed the little dog with an eyedropper four days and nights, and he lasted out the season. She wasn't ready to follow Dahkarova, not yet. Too old for some roles, she was still unique, the greatest dramatic ballerina. One new ballet designed just for her and she could hold on. How long? And then what? She looked at Emilia's eager, worshiping face. A child with a special talent that in itself wasn't enough; a girl with ambitions that might never be fulfilled; an unfocused mirror image of herself decades ago. Emilia needed Emma. It was nice to be needed, nice to have the feeling of power that came with it.

"All right," Emma said. "I will coach her."

"Oh, Emma," Carolyn said. "I couldn't."

"One day, you will," Dahkarova said.

"No, it'd be too painful."

"Nonsense. I do it. Is necessary to help someone else be good like me. Or almost."

"But, Madame, you don't ... you're not ..."

"I don't what? I not what?"

Emma let Carolyn hang in midair for a moment. "I think Carolyn means you don't dance anymore, and she does."

"So? Look!" Dahkarova pointed imperially to a photograph on the wall behind her. "Kchessinskaya. Prima ballerina of the Maryinsky! Mistress of the czar! But very good teacher."

"Like you," Emma said.

"Correct. She teach me, in Nice, while *she* was still dancing. I teach you while *I* was still dancing. Now I teach Carolyn; soon you, Emilia—*if* you work. All learn from Kchessinskaya and the Maryinsky ..."

The grand old lady always grabbed for the spotlight she still missed. And this time, in this company, it was rightfully hers: accent or no, who could relate the historical tale of the elements of ballet being passed from one dancer to another with more authority, with more relish? Her listeners enjoyed her entrancing enjoyment as she explained how the traditions had continued and lasted. Like all traditions, by being passed along from one person to another, and another, and another.

Waiting for the tea to brew, Deedee leaned against the sink, an eavesdropper. Her eyes went to the faded photograph of Kchessinskaya on the wall, then traveled over the four generations of dancers sitting around the table: Dahkarova, who had once been; Emma, who was fading out; Carolyn, who was coming in; Emilia, who was starting up. There was less than six feet between the sink and the table, but to Deedee the distance was six thousand miles, twenty years, infinite. The distance between her and a world she had once studied so hard for, worked so hard for, wanted so badly to be part of; a world she now had no real part in at all. It was all she had given up and lost.

She poured the tea and served the dancers. Then she made a place for herself next to Emilia.

Chapter Five

"Sold out," Michael reported to Adelaide, and waited.

She didn't disappoint him. "How many standees?"

"More than the limit. The Fire Department—"

"—can go to hell." Her eyes flashed merrily.

As they took their seats in the dress circle, he put his arm about her affectionately, and was shocked how frail she was getting. What in God's name the company would do after she went, he didn't know any more than he knew how much longer this maddening, magnificent woman would last. Or how she managed to watch, cajole, and manipulate every single member of the huge company for what she determined from on high was the company's good. Or how she still found time to wheedle contributions, beg for grants, scrounge up rescue money the last split second before the company went down under a sea of bills for the third time. Early this rehearsal season, they hadn't even been able to pay for new toe shoes!

Her trust fund was squeezed dry. She invariably fluttered her "Oh, dearies" and breast-stroked through troubled waters, but Michael could always tell when sinking was a real, terrifying possibility: she brought her lunch to the office in a paper bag. ("You can at least afford a lunch box," he protested once. "Too ostentatious," she replied seriously.) At those times, she made red-ink lists of deadwood that should have been cut away long before. Of course, she then delegated him hatchet man—as with Emma. And he knew she was going to demand more cutting there. No ... she would have to do it herself.

From where he was sitting, he could see Emma's lovely profile as she turned to Freddie. She had giggled when she told him how she'd bludgeoned poor Freddie to get him to this first *Giselle* of the season.

"You know, he's more afraid of me than he is of Annabelle? He said, 'Annabelle's giving a sit-down dinner,' and I said, 'Freddie, I don't give a damn. You can run off to her bloody party the minute the last curtain hits the floor. But nobody is going to say you and I are hiding. We are going together, and we are both going to look so smashing, everybody is going to ask why *we* aren't up there!' "

She did look smashing; and when Sevilla made her first entrance, she applauded precisely the right amount of time with precisely the right amount of volume. She looked as se-

Shirley MacLaine as Deedee.

Anne Bancroft as Emma.

Backstage: the long-awaited reunion between Deedee and Emma, as Deedee's husband Wayne (Tom Skerritt) and son (Phillip Saunders) watch with relief.

In Emma's dressing room. "Can you believe how young we look?"

Wayne and Deedee toast each other at their party for old ballet friends.

Deedee and Emma avoid friction over the turning point in their lives.

At the party, the young Russian dancer Yuri (Mikhail Baryshnikov) plays his guitar.

Wayne laughs at Deedee's refusal to admit she wants to accompany Emilia to New York.

At Mme. Dahkarova's Carnegie Hall apartment, Emma and Deedee compare their lives.

Dahkarova (Alexandra Danilova) explains tradition to Emilia (Leslie Browne) and Carolyn (Starr Danias).

The beginning of a love affair between Yuri (Mikhail Baryshnikov) and Emilia (Leslie Browne).

Deedee runs into Joe Rosenfeld (Anthony Zerbe), a musical conductor and would-be lover from her past.

Emma offers to give up her career for her longtime wealthy but married lover, Carter (Marshall Thompson).

"I've been taking the pill. Just in case."

A tipsy Emilia pretends to be a Russian ballerina for two boys from out-of-town.

Brilliant dance star Mikhail Baryshnikov makes his screen debut as Yuri. Above, with Marianna Tcherkassky. Below, with Antoinette Sibley as Sevilla.

Arnold (Danny Levans), Deedee, and Michael (James Mitchell) applaud Emilia in Arnold's new ballet.

"Isn't it wonderful? Aren't you exicted?"

At a Gala party, Adelaide Payton (Martha Scott) to Michael: "Even Emma has to move on. Like all the rest of us."

Emma bows to Emilia.

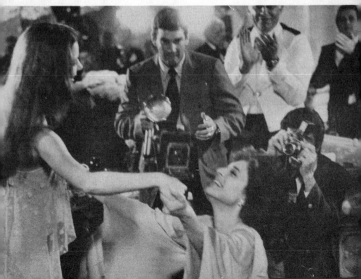

Deedee and Emma confront one another and finally slug it out.

"Daddy and I've been away from each other all summer. Sometimes when you miss someone. . ."

Deedee and Wayne finally admit the truth about their marriage as Emilia watches.

The result of Emilia's choice at her turning point.

Deedee and Emma make peace with their lives—and one another.

renē as though she were royalty at a command performance, establishment at a social event. Well, the first *Giselle* was traditionally an event, a money-maker, and sometimes a ballerina maker.

Carolyn, farther along in the same row as Emma, listening attentively to Peter's whispered comments, was certainly well aware of that. Without hearing a word, Michael could have repeated verbatim what Peter was pointing out to Carolyn about Sevilla: the movements Carolyn could copy, the movements she had to do her own way. Between Peter and Dahkarova, Carolyn would get where she was determined to get. A paradigm of ambition, she was a beauty and a beautiful dancer; and dumb as she was, she had an animal instinct for the best trainer. Plus animal strength and obedience to accomplish whatever her trainer asked. With Peter's help, *Giselle* would make Carolyn a ballerina. And break Emma.

For a bitter moment, Michael resented Peter, who gave him what Emma never would. Or never could. But it was Michael himself who had taught Peter that personal feelings, whether affection or lust, always had to take a back seat. So Peter, who laughed with Emma and found Carolyn a boring idiot, was simply doing his job; and Michael, who had done his own hurtful job, was a fool who could not stop Emma's clock. The company needed Carolyn to take Emma's place and move into second position behind Sevilla. And Sevilla's years were numbered: she was thirty-five. The whole traditional procession suddenly depressed and angered Michael. That was as foolish as being depressed and angered by life. The procession in ballet was merely life speeded up. *Giselle* would go on and on making ballerinas and breaking ballerinas.

Emma had never liked the first act of *Giselle* except for the mad scene: the peasant dancers were much too coy, and the mime defeated anyone who wasn't either a bad actress or a retarded child. Still, no one became a ballerina, not a prima ballerina, without conquering the classics—no matter what new adventures in ballet. Even after nineteen opening-night curtain calls for her *Anna Karenina,* she'd had to prove herself in *Giselle* and *Swan Lake.* And she had, triumphantly.

Be satisfied, she told herself. Michael and Adelaide are right: you're too old for Giselle, you'd be ridiculous, grotesque as a village virgin. And you can't do the thirty-two *fouettés* demanded of the Black Swan Queen, you can't do *Swan Lake* anymore, either. She'd seen too many aging ballerinas make pathetic fools of themselves clinging to both roles, and had wondered angrily why someone didn't tell them: For your own sake, stop! Don't destroy the memory!

Her eyes blurred: her past glory, her life really, trickled away like the tears sliding down her cheeks. Casually she flicked them off, pressed her eyelids as though she were smoothing her eye shadow. She turned to Freddie to see if he had noticed. His face was bleak terror. Gently she patted his hand, squeezed it, smiled and forced him to smile back, then forced herself to concentrate on the stage.

As good as Sevilla was, she was having to push to hold her own with Yuri, who was not only better, but so much younger. The evening was Yuri's, but Emma knew that when they took their bows, Sevilla would graciously make it seem that she had deliberately allowed it to be. Thus, it would end up *their* evening. Sevilla knew the tricks, just as Emma did.

The little tricks were something else she would have to teach Emilia. At the right moment, though; the girl was a purist. The little solo she was doing now in the second act: if she angled her body just a trifle upstage, that extension would be breathtaking. And if she held it a beat longer ... But she did! Deedee must have taught her that one. Good. There was no point in waiting; there wasn't time, anyway. Time was always the enemy. Talented as she was, Emilia needed to be pushed, to be taught every damn thing Emma knew, and fast.

Deedee, leaning against the left wall of the auditorium, watched Emilia proudly even as she remembered herself and Emma. It was thanks to Emma that she could walk in free any performance she wanted. But it was also thanks to Emma that she was standing out front instead of being onstage—no, by this time, at her age, she would be sitting out front like Emma, without a daughter to watch. And her daughter was good, really good. As good as she had been at that age? Memory was not to be trusted. Besides, their look, their bodies, their styles were so different. Probably Emilia was better than she had been. But then, she had never really been sure how good she was. Oh, Adelaide, Michael, everyone had told her she was wonderful, was certain to become a ballerina; fine, great, terrific. But the actual moment of proof had never come, so she never knew what she might have been. She still didn't know. Thanks to Emma.

And when she got backstage after the performance, Emma was there ahead of her. Sevilla and Yuri were still taking bows.

"Fourteen! Wow!" The stage manager counted.

The small closed-circuit television screen above his desk showed Sevilla and Yuri bowing in front of the gold house curtain. She took a flower from her bouquet and presented it to Yuri. The audience cheered her generosity; Sevilla smiled like a queen; Yuri knelt to her. More cheering, and they ran off prettily. Behind the curtain, they waited, unsmiling, sweating, gasping; Sevilla complaining about her bad right foot, Yuri clutching his bad back. The cheering grew louder; they put their pretty smiles back on and hastened out for another bow.

From the end of the little corridor leading into the wings, Deedee saw Emma standing alone by the stage manager's desk, smiling carefully. The smile made Deedee ache. She started forward, but Adelaide and Michael swept past on their way to the stage and the stars. She wanted them to stop and say something, anything, to Emma. Adelaide hurried on to kiss Sevilla and Yuri, who were back behind the curtain again; but Michael—thank God for Michael—stopped and kissed Emma very gently on the cheek, then became artistic director again and proceeded to the stage.

Deedee went to Emma and put her arm around her. "I liked the movie better."

Emma laughed. "They were incredible."

"Terrific. Hey, where does Emilia dress?"

"Let me congratulate them, and I'll show you. You should be very proud."

"Oh, you know how mothers are," Deedee said too quickly.

"Let's take her to a really fancy supper."

"No, let us take you."

Emma shook her head. "No. I want champagne."

Emilia put down the menu. "It's so expensive," she whispered.

"It's an occasion." Emma lifted her champagne. "To you."

"I'll drink to that," Deedee said.

"No," Emilia said, loving it, loving the quietly elegant room. She'd heard that Balanchine always had supper here, and there he was, with two very young, very lovely dancers. And there was Baryshnikov, and Gelsey Kirkland, and Sevilla with the Englishman who had flown over just to see her.

"I feel sorry for Carolyn," Emilia said.

"You mean having to follow Sevilla?" Emma asked.

"Well, yes, but really because she won't have Yuri to partner her. He's so beautiful." She blushed. "As a dancer. He's the best I've ever seen in my whole life. The best male dancer, I mean," she added quickly, looking at Emma.

"Did you watch him tonight?" Deedee asked.

"Oh, yes!" Emilia's eyes were shining. "I was in the wings every chance I had. I meant to watch Sevilla—like you told me to," she said to Emma, "but I couldn't help looking at him. He makes it all seem so easy. His body is so strong, and yet he ... he seems to float. Sometimes, when the light catches his hair, or his arms go out to you, or you suddenly see his eyes ... he's just beautiful." She heard herself, and looked down at her plate.

Her mother and her godmother looked at each other.

"Oh, dear," Deedee said softly, remembering, and, like Emma, feeling ancient.

Two days later, life was behaving like life, offering change and surprise. The air was warm, not hot, the city sparkled, and Deedee felt like a girl. In the morning she met with Adelaide and got her job set at the school; in the afternoon, to celebrate, she took both Emilia and Ethan to Bloomingdale's basement. Then, coming home, walking up Fifty-seventh Street, a big dancing bear of a man came out of the Russian Tea Room, sneaked up behind Deedee, and whirled her around in his arms. She let out a shriek, and the kids gaped. The bear set her down, and she looked at him with delight.

"Rosie!"

"Who else?" he asked.

He had a swooping mustache and maestro hair now, but his clothes were as careless as ever, and his crinkling eyes were as warm as they had been twenty years ago. She introduced the kids and tried to explain who Joe Rosenfeld was while he bowed to Emilia and saluted Ethan like the hired clown at a children's party. They thought he was ridiculous, but were careful not to show it; he was vulnerable and needed protection.

"Rosie used to conduct for the company when Daddy and I were dancing," Deedee explained. "He was the best."

"Still am," Rosie said. "Only I conduct musi-

cals now. More bread and a permanent pad."
He winked at Emilia, who giggled to make him
happy. "Where you heading, cutie?" he asked
Deedee.

"We live up the block."

He took her shopping bag, and linking arms,
started her walking up the street.

"How's your wife?" she asked loudly for the
benefit of Emila and Ethan.

"Which one? I've had two since I last saw
you."

"All three."

"Dynamite. I never see them. How's your
hubby?"

"Home in Oklahoma City with our other
daughter. I'm just here for the summer."

"Terrific!"

He hugged her close, making her more delightedly nervous. She would have been even if
the children weren't there.

"This is where we get off," she said. They had
reached the entrance to her building.

"Okay," Rosie boomed. "I'm loose!"

He walked in with her, carrying her shopping bag as though it were his suitcase. Ethan
and Emilia followed like watchdogs, unsure
now who needed protection.

In Oklahoma City in midsummer, the Rogers
School of Ballet had very few children of the
Nichols Hills rich. Most of Wayne's pupils
came from families who went up to Grand

Lake (of the Cherokees) in the northeastern part of the state for weekends. Nichols Hills families moved to lakes in Minnesota and Michigan. The Fernbachers owned a house in Michigan, but Ken Fernbacher had come back to town. Oil and Arabs, he explained vaguely to Wayne. He had taken to dropping by after Wayne's last class to split a beer, suggesting they have dinner together downtown, maybe tie one on. He knew Wayne must be lonely, he said. Wayne thanked him, but Janina had fixed dinner, and he explained he didn't want *her* to be lonely (not saying that the minute the dishes were washed, Janina was out and off with her friends).

He knew, of course, what Ken was really suggesting, and he resented the implication about male ballet dancers even though he knew it was largely justified. Even more, though, he resented men like Ken Fernbacher who couldn't face or accept their sexuality, whatever it was. It made them furtive, not open; it made Ken suggest, not ask. Oklahomans read about sexual variety, even talked about it, but as though it were a condition special to New York and California. They had been at all of it when Wayne left town as a boy, they were still at all of it now, and always would be. But then and now, they pretended they weren't; or that they were drunk; or that they were men together, and what the hell, with their old ladies away, it was better than picking up some hooker or somebody else's wife, who would only open her big mouth and blab, and so forth and so on. Maybe the women with their empty afternoons and their new best girlfriends were more open; maybe they had to pretend-drink—why did they always go to the john in pairs? And what would the mouths say if men did that?

Ken Fernbacher persisted without obviously pushing. He had the kind of assurance that is special to the rich, the self-confidence that is special to the physically attractive. His lazy drawl went with his long, lean, relaxed body, and his charm was more than a smile showing white teeth in a suntanned face. It was even more than the use of subtle flattery—which he was very good at. It was showing need.

"Funny how easy it is for me to talk to you," he said to Wayne as they sat drinking boilermakers in his very masculine game room.

It was a Saturday night, and Wayne had run out of excuses. Moreover, the Fernbachers were important in rich Nichols Hills, and the Nichols Hills rich were important to Wayne's livelihood. So he told himself, and it was true; but it was also true he felt the flutterings of an excitement he hadn't felt in years.

"It's easier for me to say some things to you than it is to my wife," Ken said. "Why is that?"

"Oh, sometimes it's easier to talk to a stranger."

"Come on. You're no stranger. I wish you were, though."

"Why?"

Ken looked up, longing scrawled all over his face. "Because then I wouldn't feel about you the way I do feel," he said casually. "And don't tell me you don't know what that is because you do. And you feel it yourself."

They were each sprawled in a big leather club chair at opposite ends of a long coffee table.

"I feel like I've been drinking too much," Wayne said and put his glass down.

"Let's take a swim."

Wayne could see the pool gleaming softly just beyond the big bay windows. He wanted a swim: he wanted to feel cool water slip around his naked body; part of him even wanted what he knew would happen in the pool and after. Since Deedee, he had not been with a man, but if there was Ken Fernbacher tonight, there would be others. And then he would be lost.

He looked at his watch and stood up. "I'd love a swim, but I've got to pick up Janina," he lied, and left, feeling guilty anyway. Because, to an extent, he had led Ken on. Which made him feel once again that he was as much of a hypocrite as anyone in town. Once again, over and over, for years and years, all their years—for not only had he never cleared up that subject with Deedee, he had never even mentioned it. Not once. He'd always been, he still was, too ashamed. The result was a wall of silence between them.

If she were there now, he could talk to her, tell her. He missed her terribly; he was lonelier than he had ever thought he could be. In twenty years, he had not had any woman, either, except Deedee. Not because they were always together, but because he had never wanted anyone else for more than two minutes. Once he had gotten what he felt was the best— and he knew that, for him, Deedee was—he was satisfied and content. He had no need for conquest, no desire for the hunt. He had no ambitions.

But he was a dancer, physical, conscious of bodies, and Ken Fernbacher's suggestions reached into his loneliness and stirred his sexuality. Not in Ken's direction, because he didn't dare, but in the direction of Donna Michaels, who was in his summer class for adults. Really a glorified exercise class for women who were mainly youngish, overweight, and frustrated. Donna was youngish, too blond, smoked incessantly, had an incredible body, and was not frustrated. She was greedy, however, and she wanted Wayne. Adept enough to make that clear without anyone noticing, she was also patient, and made it equally clear that sooner or later, she would get him. He was afraid she would. Being from Oklahoma, he felt guilty in advance. In desperation, he told her she couldn't take class if she continued to smoke in the studio. She nodded and took cigarette breaks in the office, where Janina had taken over Deedee's bookkeeping. Donna liked a little challenge now and then.

Embarrassed as she felt her nipples harden under her thin leotard, Emilia forced herself to look where she should be looking: at the reflections in the mirrored wall of Sevilla, Carolyn, and herself, all executing the same movements from the balcony scene of MacMillan's *Romeo and Juliet*. Except that Sevilla, as usual, was smoking and chattering away to Yuri, her Romeo, while she rehearsed. She even muttered a running commentary on stage while she danced: it helped her, and her partners simply had to get used to it.

Although Sevilla was getting too old for Juliet, the ballet was being put into the repertoire to please her; she had had enormous success with it at Covent Garden. Carolyn, who would dance the ballet only at occasional matinees, was working with a new partner who had been brought into the company to please *her*: Francisco Morales, as young as Yuri, an amazing technician, acted like a silent screen star who produced his own pictures, but—and Michael and Adelaide had sighed with relief— he was much taller than Carolyn even when she was on pointe.

Emilia, the only one of the three Juliets young enough for the part, was merely the understudy in case tendonitis or temperament struck simultaneously. Her Romeo, Clark Schafer, was as promising a dancer as she was. Younger than Yuri, blonder than Yuri, handsomer and better built than Yuri, he always wore white in rehearsal and a self-knitted cloche hat. Everyone in the company—and they would know, just as they had known in the days of Wayne and Deedee—said he was straight. It didn't matter to Emilia. She wouldn't have cared anyway; but although she liked to dance with Clark, when she looked at him, she saw Yuri.

All during rehearsal, she had been dancing with Yuri. In the mirror she had sought his eyes, his arms, the bulge in his tights. He was her Romeo, she was his Juliet, she was anything he wanted.

All three couples were balanced in the same embrace now. Sevilla, turning her head to the mirror to see if it caught her perfection, exhaled a cloud of smoke in Yuri's face. He turned his head and saw Emilia, saw what was in her eyes. He smiled slightly; she blushed. As they continued to dance, he began to dance with her, to be her Romeo in the mirror, to hold her, to want her. And she knew it.

A boy and a girl, each dancing with someone else in the room; in the mirror, dancing with each other. The other dancers, the ballet master, the pianist, disappear; even the room, the walls, disappear. Only the music remains, the music and the girl falling in love with the boy, and the boy falling in love with the reflected figures in the mirrored wall.

There was no point in turning on the light to look at the clock again. It wouldn't bring Emilia home any quicker, any more than it would tell her where Emilia was. Anyway, Deedee was sure she knew where Emilia was. The few times Emilia went out after a performance with kids like Sandra, who dressed next to her, or Clark, who probably had some sort of crush on her, she was always home and in the other twin bed at a reasonably early hour. Instinct as well as the hour told Deedee with whom her daughter was, where she was, what she was doing. For the first time.

She hoped it would be good for Emilia. It would certainly be good for Emilia's hang-up on Wayne.... Well, it might be difficult for Wayne. Abruptly, it was difficult for her. Her mind whirled with upsetting pictures of Emilia and Yuri, herself and Wayne, herself and Rosie, Emilia frightened, Emilia in tears, Emilia's young body, and her own aging body.

She sat up to turn on the bed lamp, then heard the front door open carefully, quickly switched off the light, and slid down on the pillow, praying Emilia hadn't been hurt and wouldn't be hurt. She heard her tiptoe down the hall, then into their room.

"You can turn on the light," Deedee said, careful to keep her voice soft and pleasant.

"I didn't mean to wake you." No nervousness.

"You didn't." Deedee sat up and put on the lamp.

Emilia was glowing. "I was with Yuri."

"Are you okay?"

"Oh, yes! I've been taking the pill." Emilia smiled, and looked sixteen, even now. "Just in case."

"Good God."

"So there's nothing to worry about. Go to sleep now."

That was going to be all? "Don't you want to talk?"

"It might spoil it," Emilia said dreamily. "Sleep well."

She went into the bathroom to undress, closing the door and leaving Deedee feeling she wasn't a mother, wasn't being allowed to be a mother. Wasn't necessary. The damn kid didn't know what had happened to her! Or maybe it hadn't. She got out of bed and hurried to take Emilia into her arms.

"Emilia!"

She opened the bathroom door. Emilia was brushing her teeth. Deedee waited til she finished, then held out her arms.

"Emilia," she said again.

"Be glad for me, Mama." Emilia gently pushed her back toward bed.

"Glad?!"

"Yes. Go to sleep now." *She* sounded like the mother!

"I am glad, only . . ." She let Emilia lead her back toward her bed. "Well, I didn't think it'd be so soon that you . . ."

"That I what?" Emilia teased.

"Ohhhh." Deedee smiled ruefully. "That you wouldn't just want to dance."

In the morning Emilia raced through her usual breakfast, kissed Deedee, Dahkarova and even Ethan, and tore out of the house. Yuri was waiting down in the street, holding his practice bag. She smiled tenderly at him, he smiled back, and she burst into laughter: he had blacked out all his teeth.

From the window, Deedee watched them walk down the street laughing, each holding a practice bag, each holding the other's hand. When they reached the corner, they stopped and kissed. She became aware that the telephone was ringing and nobody was going to answer unless she did. It was Rosie. Would she meet him after his show? Yes; sure; why not? New York was marvelous.

Chapter Six

Emma and her partner danced like lovers, which they were. With her shimmering new dress, she wore the diamond earrings he had given her, as well as the diamond necklace and ring he had also given her. He wore black tie with ease; he was even at ease in white tie. They were the most attractive couple on the floor.

The music, played by a restrained jazz quintet, was good for dancing; the floor wasn't. It was stone, the floor of the Tapesty Gallery of the Metropolitan Museum of Art, the night's setting for yet another charity dinner dance. The confident wife of Emma's partner was involved in a great many charities. She was also rather fond of ballet, and often invited Emma who usually managed to cajole Michael into escorting her. Last year, the parties were in the department stores; this year, it was museums: fewer people, but richer; better food, but a higher tariff; the same amount of profit, however, and the same lack of excitement for all but the few diehard romantics still hoping the White Horse would arrive, either with the Knight or Godiva. Emma attended to establish publicly that she was friendly with Carter's wife as well as with Carter.

His hand played lightly with her back as he talked about his children. Emma was charming, taking as much care with what she said as she had with how she looked.

"And Linda's been accepted at Yale," Carter said.

"I guess nobody wants to go to Princeton anymore."

"Obviously not my kids. All five pick different schools, but not one picks my alma mater. Would you say that's a reflection on me?"

"No, Carter, I'd say that's a reflection on Princeton."

"You're biased."

"Oh, for years."

"I can't kiss you here."

"It wouldn't upset me."

"It might upset Maggie."

"Enough to give you a divorce?" She stopped dancing to intercept a passing waiter. "May I?" She took a glass of champagne from the tray for each of them.

"I'd only have to ask for a divorce, Emma. You know that."

"Well?" she asked as though she hadn't rehearsed for the conversation.

"Would you give up dancing?"

"Why not?" She waved hello to someone across the room.

"I asked you fifteen years ago, fourteen years—"

"Ask me now."

He signaled a waitress. "I'll have one of those cheese things. Thank you." She knew then she should drop it, should give up. "Emma, you know one of the reasons we've lasted so long?"

He was the only man who consistently aroused her in bed. "Tell me another."

"The whole arrangement has suited you," Carter said. From the beginning, that had been another surprise: his directness. "You liked the limitations."

"I don't think I do anymore." She managed to keep her voice very even.

"But now I do," he said gently, regretfully, because he remembered loving her, and still cared. "I'm sorry." He was, also consistently, a very nice man.

"So am I." She said it like a parting kiss. They stood, sipping champagne, not knowing what else to do.

Then Carter said, "Would you rather I didn't come by later?"

In bed, he might change his mind. But she knew him well enough to know that was absurd. She thought of her apartment, with everything in its proper place; of her three little dogs; of her large bed. "No, come by." She laughed. "We might as well finish out the season."

He led her back to their table, where she sat down next to Michael.

"You look particularly beautiful tonight," he said, not complimenting, appraising shrewdly.

"That was the general idea." She held out her glass for more champagne, wondering whether it would have worked out with him, whether their lives would have been very different. "Where's Peter?"

Michael shrugged.

"Does it matter?"

Michael shook his head. "No. Whatever he's doing, it's fine by both of us."

"That's good," Emma said, and meant it.

Like everyone in the company, Emma knew Emilia was having an affair with Yuri. Having watched Yuri pick up and let down one girl after another from the moment he came into the company, she wanted to talk to Emilia, but distrusted her own motives. Were she Emilia, not only would she resent advice, it wouldn't be necessary. As it was, she was moving in on the most important part of Emilia's life anyway—her dancing—and Emilia was dancing better than ever.

If Emilia needed to be warned, the person to do it was Deedee. But it was difficult for Emma to get hold of Deedee. She taught a good part of the day; at night, Emma was performing;

and after her performance, Deedee was too often with Rosie. Emma had after-theater supper with them once and suspected they were having an affair, too. If they weren't, it obviously wasn't Rosie's fault.

Deedee said nothing to anyone about Rosie, though she didn't keep him a secret. She had him to the apartment, and when she was going to have supper with him after his show, made sure Emilia and Ethan knew it. She also made sure she got home before Emilia did.

Emilia was in that state of total egocentricity: love. Nothing registered, nothing mattered except Yuri and dancing. Dancing because he was a dancer and she wanted to dance, not as well as he, because that was impossible for anyone on her earth, but well enough to be able to dance with him. She was happy in class, happier in performance, happiest at night in his apartment where they did little else beyond making love. It was what he wanted to do, so it was what she wanted to do. Besides, his English wasn't very good.

Still, she always reached the point when she would jump out of bed and get dressed to go home. She herself didn't quite understand why she had to go home, why she was doing it now.

"Really, you are crazy," Yuri said. "Stay!"

"My mother would have a fit."

"Then she is also crazy."

"She's just a very proper lady." She looked at him, sprawled out on the bed, his naked body partly covered by a sheet. He grinned at her, flicked back the sheet: he had an erection again. She turned away, but he grabbed her, threw her down on the bed, started to unzip her dress.

"Yuri, I can't!"

"Yes."

"*Nyet!*"

"*Da!*" His hands were doing what he knew she liked.

"Half an hour," she said, shuddering.

"No. All night." He stopped touching her and lay back. He was so quiet, she could hardly hear him. "Please."

"Why?"

He turned his head away. It was difficult for him to ask anything, more difficult for him to put what he felt into English. "Homesick," he said at last.

Gently she touched him with one finger, kissed his hair lightly, took off her clothes, and cradled him in her arms.

Deedee made one rule: they all had to have the evening meal together at Dahkarova's. Emilia and Ethan could invite anyone they wanted (if they gave her enough notice), but they had to be there. Dinner had to be early so Emilia could get to the theater in time to warm up before performance. That suited Rosie because he liked to arrive early at the Broadway theater where he was conducting. He began to seem too much a part of the family, so Deedee invited Michael and Peter, to Dahkarova's delight. She liked her dining table crowded, so long as she didn't have to cook or wash up.

"You give up ballet to conduct Broadway?" she said pityingly to Rosie. "You are man without soul."

"You are woman without wine." He refilled her glass.

"He bring this wine?" Dahkarova asked.

"Yep," Deedee said proudly.

"Well, taste he got." The old lady turned her guns on Michael now. "You, darling, have much soul—"

"But not much taste." Michael laughed.

"Correct," Dahkarova said.

"You both owe me an apology," Peter said, as the telephone rang.

"I'll get it!" Emilia and Ethan said together, he mimicking her perfectly. She ran into the hall without blushing. Everyone except Dahkarova laughed.

"Ethan." She wagged her finger at him. "Is honor for Emilia."

"Honor?" Deedee was indignant.

"*Da.* Yuri is best dancer I see in years."

"Of course, my dear," Michael said. "He's Russian."

"Correct. When I was young girl—"

"Come on, Dahkarova, you can't remember that far back."

"Mischa, darling, *that* time is very clear. So

clear like today. In between is not clear. Well, in between, I am very ... busy." She smiled coyly. "Like Deedee."

Neither Deedee nor Ethan laughed.

"I don't get the joke," Ethan said. "What's the joke, Rosie?"

Rosie imitated Dahkarova's Russian accent. "It don't translate, kid." But he looked anxiously at Deedee.

She jumped up and got very busy clearing the table, like a good mother. Dahkarova had never made a joke like that before because there was no basis for the inference. Now there was, and somehow she knew it. How? How was it people always knew, sensed, whatever, that two people were having sex? It was too easy to say that they behaved differently before and after, and it wasn't always true. Deedee had known Michael and Peter were sexual mates the moment she saw them, which was before she knew that they were lovers.

It didn't bother her that Dahkarova knew, or Michael or Peter. Or Emma. The night Emma had supper with her and Rosie, Emma obviously caught on; that was O.K. She'd even been rather glad. She herself hadn't been bothered, probably because she'd been brought up in the ballet world, where sex was free and easy, maybe too easy. Well, Rosie was a good man, and good in bed. One of the dreams she'd had about coming to New York was a thing with a man like Rosie. An over-forty dream, accentuated by twenty years of going to bed with only one man. In Oklahoma City.

Still, she'd been very careful. She didn't want Wayne to know, or the children. The thing with Rosie had meaning only for her: it reassured her she was alive and desirable; gave her a pride and contentment; made her better with herself, which made her better for Wayne and the kids. So she thought, yet wouldn't go to bed with Rosie that night. And the next morning, at breakfast, and later, at the school, watched Ethan to see if he behaved any differently to her, if he suspected, if he knew.

Thinking about it as she taught one of her own classes, she felt resentment because she suddenly felt guilt. Oklahoma City? Or was guilt inevitable, a natural state? But what she had with Rosie was natural. And just before, watching Ethan do a combination, she had heard him say "Oh, shit!" when he fell. That was natural. But then, an older boy—fifteen!— had picked Ethan up and hugged him. Was that natural? Should she let Ethan stay in the ballet, and if she did, what would happen to him sexually, and would *that* be natural?

Ethan mustn't know, that was clear and important. Emilia was too immersed in Yuri to be aware, but if she found out, Deedee could explain it to her, and she would understand. Particularly now that her overattachment to her father was ended. And Wayne ... Well, how would she feel if Wayne were going to bed with someone in Oklahoma City? Not with Ken Fernbacher; Wayne wouldn't. He probably wouldn't with one of those hungry mothers, either, but she hoped he was. Because she was with Rosie? Wayne would know why, Wayne would understand. A sudden, almost desperate need for him made her tremble. She felt unsafe, insecure, anxious. The thing with Rosie, the affair—it *was* an affair—was trouble; and trouble, like furtiveness, didn't titillate her. The affair was soiled, spoiled; it should end. She would have to dump darling Rosie.

Yuri would have understood Deedee and Rosie completely. What he wouldn't have understood was Deedee and Wayne. Twenty years of fidelity? Why? Boring; also impossible; also unbelievable.

He sat on the floor of Carolyn's dressing room massaging her ankle. She had fallen while they were rehearsing. The stage manager hurrying by the open door stopped to ask how Carolyn was. If she wasn't going to be able to perform tonight, he wanted to know now. As usual, once the goddamn season was underway, too many of the dancers were out with goddamn torn ligaments, sprains, fractures—Christ, you name it.

"Oh, she is better," Yuri said.

"Much," Carolyn said. "I'll be on tonight."

"Thanks." The stage manager hurried away.

Yuri continued to knead Carolyn's ankle.

"That feels so good," she said. "It was my fault."

"No."

"Yes. I was so nervous." Her voice rose like a child's.

"Why?"

"You're so fabulous, and I'm so tall."

"I like tall girls." Yuri's hands moved up to massage her calf.

"You just like girls."

He grinned. "Very much. Is wrong?"

"Oh, no! I personally think everyone should have the right to make their own choice," Carolyn said generously. She leaned forward. "I like yours."

"My what?"

"Your choice."

He was totally confused. "Is my English."

"No, it's mine. I have such difficulty—"

"Carolyn." His hands were sliding up her leg now. "Sometimes is better not to talk."

"Oh, I agree," she said enthusiastically. "People just go on and on, and nobody understands what—"

"Carolyn." He kissed her knee and looked up at her.

She leaned back. Her eyes changed, and when she spoke, her voice was sexual and decisive. "Yes."

He opened her robe, and kissing her thigh, reached out with one leg to close the door. It swung shut a little too slowly because there was time for Emilia, who was passing by, to look in and see them.

Wayne was very late for supper, and Janina was proud of her cooking. As he set the table, she made a great show of turning the stove burners up and down, down and up—Joan at the stake, building her own fires, obviously destined for burning. She didn't ask questions, nor did she overtly connect Donna Michaels with Wayne, but her pointed monologue made it clear where she stood and how much she would stand for.

"She waltzes into the office every five minutes and blows smoke from those stinking cigarettes practically down my throat. I feel like *I* ought to give up smoking. And that hair! I have absolutely no objection to dyed blonde, Daddy, but she *could* do it with some subtlety and taste, not that trashy, obvious—"

"All right," Wayne said sharply. "Cool it."

Full of remorse over her probably unnecessary attempted homicide, Janina turned from the stove and went to Wayne. He said nothing, just continued to set the table. She looked at it: he had set places for three and was starting on the fourth.

"Oh, Daddy," she said sadly.

He looked at the table. "Just keeping in practice," he said, and hugged her.

Deedee took off her shoes and got two beers

from the wood-paneled fridge while Rosie hunted among his albums for the right record. The moonlight streaming through the big skylight of his SoHo loft looked as though he had sent out for it. She turned on a lamp they didn't need.

"Oh, I had the hots for you back then," Rosie was saying. "Only back then I didn't look so good in tights. Now the toe shoe is on the other foot."

"Oh, is it?"

"Yeah. Now we both don't look so good in tights."

"Speak for yourself." She laughed.

"I am," he said, suddenly very serious.

She was sure now what was coming. She had sensed it almost from the moment she had picked him up at the stage door of his theater. Rosie's face was as open as his loft which, except for the bathroom, had no walls or doors. Space was divided by shelves of books and records and by sculptured partitions he had built himself. Like Wayne, he was good with his hands.

"I could open up new vistas for you, cutie."

His use of vaudeville for protection was so obvious it always touched her. And made it harder for her to say no. Which he knew, of course. "Rosie—"

"Listen," he interrupted, "dancers are ignorant. What do you know? Ballet and kids."

"What do you know? Music and divorce."

"One moment for station identification, please." He pointed to his shelves. "Books!" He threw a newspaper into the air. "Corruption!" He pointed to abstract paintings. "Dirty pictures!" He made a little-boy bow. "Divorce is a bummer, violets are blue, music is great . . . and so are you."

"That's very nice," she said gently. "Oh, Rosie, I've got the guilts."

"You're human. Simple way to end 'em."

"Yes, but not your way. You've got them, too."

"Me? The original free soul? What guilts 've I got?"

"Whatever guilts, Rosie darling, that make you feel you have to marry the girl you're having an affair with."

"Who says I want to marry you?"

"Nobody." She went for her shoes.

He sat helplessly on the big marble coffee table. "Back in the Icebox Age, I had an apartment on West Fifty-second Street. You left before the best part . . . You don't remember."

She didn't. "I remember it was over a jazz joint."

"Don't leave now." He was looking at the floor, but he could hear she had stopped moving. He raised his eyes to hers. "You know why it *is* the best part?" No answer. He grinned anxiously. "Because it gets you off your feet." She smiled. "I'll put on *Sleeping Beauty*," he coaxed, and jumped up and did an adorably awkward arabesque that made her laugh. She took off her shoes and stayed.

Emilia turned on her damp pillow, feeling misery strangely turn to anger as she stared at the stripe of moon on Deedee's empty bed. She was all cried out, but thankfully, Yuri had not seen a tear when she told him they'd had it. She'd stood on the corner near the theater, looking untouchable, listening coolly to his nonsense explanations, until she felt herself beginning to go. Then she had turned and walked swiftly home, letting the tears pour down but holding back her sobs until she was inside her room.

He had made it worse, pretending he couldn't understand why on earth she should care: Carolyn meant nothing to him, why should she mean anything to Emilia? Once, in the dressing room when the other girls were gossiping about affairs, she had said quietly what she thought, and Sandra said Emilia's idea of romance came from *Swan Lake.* Not true: it came from her father and mother. Her father only, she now saw. Her mother was like Yuri. Wayne was beautiful, he was love as it should be, he was the only one who was honest. He and Emma. Because Emma at least gave her love openly and honestly to dancing, and was faithful to it. Of course, in that way, she couldn't be hurt. Well, that wasn't quite true. She was being hurt now, dancing wasn't being faithful to her, but she wasn't being deceived by someone like Yuri or Deedee, who both—

The telephone rang.

She sat up. She knew it was Yuri. She let it ring. She twisted the wet rag of a handkerchief she still clutched. Then, needing to talk to him, wanting to hear his promises, tore out of bed and down the hall, frightened that the phone would stop ringing before she could get there. She picked it up, took a deep breath, then said as casually as she could, "Hello? . . . *Daddy!*"

Somehow there were more tears. She jammed the handkerchief over the phone until she was in control. "Hello? . . . I'm fine. I just dropped the phone."

In his big chair in the den, Wayne heard the shakiness behind her chatter and fixed a bright smile on his face as though she were in the room with him. "Oh, Janina's taking great care of me, and she's terrific at the school. Honey, I forgot it was so much later there." He let her prattle and prattled back, carefully trying to hear what she wasn't saying. "Yeah, Mom wrote you had the lead. Well, don't let that Arnold Berger scare you. Sic your boyfriend on him. Hey, how is he, by the way?"

Easily now, she said, "O.K. I really don't have time for that sort of thing."

Too easy: he got it, and his false smile got bigger, his voice cheerier. "I don't wonder. They always work you hard when you're really good. Say ... put Mom on for a minute, will you?"

She was prepared for this, she thought. "Oh, Momma's with Emma. They're always yakking. Sometimes she even stays over."

He looked away from the telephone, from her. "That's good." Very brightly again: "Well, tell her to call when she gets a chance. Now you get back to bed and—" And he didn't know what.

But she cut in and saved him, tears in her eyes, but not, she hoped, in her voice. "Daddy ... could you come to New York soon?"

"You bet! The minute school finishes, Janina and I are getting on a plane!"

She heard, just as he heard, and they both knew they had to hang up quickly. "I love you, Daddy," she said just once more, then put the receiver in its cradle and went back to bed.

Much later, she heard the front door open carefully and Deedee tiptoe down the hall into their room. They both pretended Emilia was asleep.

In the morning, Deedee was up first, bustling hopefully in the kitchen: breakfast was normalcy, breakfast made the world go round, breakfast was a family affair. Orange juice for everyone; bacon and eggs for Ethan; herring for Dahkarova; English muffin to be snatched from the oven as soon as Emilia appeared.

Dahkarova loved breakfast; it was her time with Ethan. The others were never talkative then, so she had him to herself, and he loved to listen to her tales. Each regarded the other as an interesting philosopher.

"So Diaghilev, he cry, and Nijinsky, he cry, too," she finished.

"Because they're Russian," Ethan said.

"Because they are happy."

"That's what I meant."

"Correct. I cry also," Dahkarova added her coda.

"How come I never see you cry now?" Ethan asked. "You look happy."

Dahkarova shrugged. "For my age. I also look good for my age.... You don't understand."

"No."

"Listen, darling. Imagine you are as old as me."

He examined her face critically, then shook his head. "I can't."

"Then I cannot explain!" she said testily.

"Good morning!" Deedee said cheerfully to Emilia who came in, carrying her practice bag.

"Up late?" Dahkarova asked hopefully.

"Daddy called last night," Emilia said. Deedee, taking the English muffin from the oven, had her back turned. "I told him you were with Emma."

"Why didn't you wake me?" Ethan demanded.

"It was very late." She drank her orange juice standing up, refused the muffin Deedee offered. "He and Janina sent you their love," she said to Ethan, and picked up her bag.

"Emilia." Deedee touched the girl's arm lightly. "What time are you having lunch today?" She was pleading.

"I'm busy," Emilia said, and left.

Dahkarova looked at Deedee who smiled and reached for the coffeepot.

"Something's funny," Ethan said.

Across the country, Janina awoke and went into the sunny kitchen to find Wayne already there. Her suspicion that something was funny was confirmed when he said he didn't want bacon and eggs, just English muffin and coffee. Then, while she was making her breakfast—she loved him, but she was still hungry—he started talking about New York.

"Wait a minute," she said. "You don't mean visit, you mean live there."

"Would you hate it?"

"How do I know?" She brought her plate to the table. "It mainly means leaving here sooner than I planned."

"What plan?"

She put down her fork. "To go to college back East. Daddy, you promised. There's gotta be one person in this family who knows something besides *Swan Lake!*"

Wayne laughed, really laughed. "Janina, I promised, and I'll keep my promise."

"How? Where're you gonna get the money?

You can't open a ballet school in New York. Too much competition. How're we going to live? How're we—?"

"Don't worry about it."

"How can I *not* worry about it?" She began to eat again, then stopped. "Listen, we better sit down and discuss this very thoroughly tonight. God knows you and I are the only ones with common sense around here."

He enjoyed watching her eat, enjoyed the early sun in their kitchen, enjoyed living in their house in Oklahoma. Janina did, too, but he knew if he said it was necessary to say good-bye and go to New York, she would say good-bye and go. She was a nice girl; he had a nice family. He couldn't visualize any existence without them. But Emilia's headquarters were New York now, and Deedee surely wanted to stay. So he was going to have to say good-bye to the house he had assumed he would always come home to.

Chapter Seven

Emilia, in rehearsal with Arnold for his new ballet, felt she had at last come into her own and was going to be a ballerina. Until today, she had worked to give whatever Arnold asked as precisely as possible, according to his changing whim. To choreographers, dancers were things, robots, bodies without head or heart, so she had never tried to do more than Arnold asked, to bring anything of her own to *his* ballet.

Yet, in the wings every night to study Sevilla and Carolyn, she had noted the differences in their equally impeccable techniques: the slightly different phrasing to the same music, the subtly different execution of the same steps, the result personal, special: a ballerina. But she had also watched Emma, and Emma, even at this shaky stage, was greater than the other two. Because Emma infused whatever she danced with an enormous injection of what she herself thought and felt, and the result was a unique individual blazing across the stage.

Today, in the mirrors of the rehearsal hall, it all came together for Emilia. Underneath the jagged, angular movements of Arnold's abstract ballet were Yuri and Deedee: love and anger, ecstasy and torment, illusion and disillusion, turbulence, desire, sex, anguish, disaster, the works. All the emotions were inside, raw and ready to be summoned by the music or the movement or both. The call came, she responded, inspired, marvelously fulfilled. This was dancing!

Arnold clapped his hands sharply. The pianist and the dancers stopped. He flashed his lighthouse smile.

"Emilia, all that emotion is terrific," he said softly. "For the mad scene in a piece of old-hat crap like *Giselle*, not for my ballet. You're not playing an uptight village virgin gone bananas. You're just occupying space. Moving in space with music. Not *to* music, *with* music. That's what dancing is. So please don't emote, Emilia. Don't think. Just move as I tell you to move, to the counts I give you. O.K.?" He smiled pleasantly.

Neither her body nor her huge eyes showed that her shocked mind was thrashing like a washing machine. No emotion, please, no honesty, no openness; not wanted, not desirable. To feel is to be hurt. "I don't count," she whispered.

"Then how do you know what to do when?"

Arnold asked. "ESP?" The other dancers studied the floor.

"I feel it—with the music," Emilia answered quietly. "And I make it fit."

Peter, standing by the piano, caught the sharp edge in Emilia's voice. Arnold didn't. "Well, don't feel it," he commanded. "Count it. Where were we, Peter?"

"Bar one-thirty-two," Peter said. "With no feeling, please."

Arnold opened his mouth, but the pianist struck the opening chords and the dancers began to move rapidly. Emilia simply stood still, staring coldly at Arnold as the dancers whirled around her. Then she walked off the floor, snatched up her sweater just as Emma had done two weeks earlier, and walked out of the rehearsal.

"Another?"

"Please." Emilia smiled sweetly at the bartender. When he returned with her manhattan, she took out the cherry and carefully placed it next to the two other pretty cherries on the nice white little cocktail napkin.

It was very pleasant sitting on the swivel stool at the end of the almost empty bar, very peaceful. Something she should do more often. The friendly room hung lazily in late-afternoon or early-evening sun—she wasn't sure which. Leaning carefully to one side so she could peer through the window, she tried to see how many theatergoers were across the street in Lincoln Center Plaza. The sun blinded her, and at the same moment, the jukebox went on. Not rock, but jazz; sweet and tender. It went nicely with her manhattan. She took a nice long comforting swallow, and the two boys who had turned on the music were next to her.

They were both about her age, scrubbed-looking with their neat, short hair and their clean sport shirts and pressed slacks. Their faces were nicely arranged. Each had the kind of face that once was considered good-looking but now was a public announcement that its owner was a square from out of town.

"Would you mind settlin' a little wager we made?" the one in the plaid shirt asked in a familiar accent. "We're from outta town, and we just know you are, too!"

Emilia squinted at him: nice boy.

"Right?" he asked.

Very nice boy.

"I knew it! Bartender! Sir? Another round here, please."

Both boys grabbed stools and settled close to Emilia.

"This here is Barney Joe from Lake Charles, Louisiana," Plaid Shirt said, "and I'm Billy Britt from Amarillo, west Texas. Where you from?"

Very nice boys; kids; children. "Leningrad. Soviet Union," Emilia said in Yuri's accent.

"You're kiddin'." Billy Britt was impressed. "What're you doin' here?"

"I am defector, I need artistic freedom."

"Hey! What are you, anyway?"

"Artist," she said gravely. "Is why I need artistic freedom."

The way she had her hair up in that funny knot, she probably was Russian. And the little bag by her stool, she told them, contained toe shoes and tights. She was a ballerina! They had lucked out. They nudged each other in shared fantasy of delights to come, and were fascinated when she delicately plucked the cherry from her new manhattan and placed it neatly next to the others on her cocktail napkin.

"Say," Billy Britt said slyly, "what're you savin' your cherries for?" He and Barney Joe giggled.

Emilia looked at them sadly. "I save them for supper." She downed half the drink and felt warm and happy, very happy with these two nice boys. They didn't belong in New York, they were too nice. They made nice jokes, and they bought her another nice drink. She wanted to be nice to them, to take care of them. Nice people belonged with nice people.

The sun was no longer exploding in the window. She could see people hurrying through traffic, lots of people crossing the street, crowds in front of the theaters in the plaza. She tossed down her drink.

"Is suppertime," she said, and ate a cherry.

Then she gave Barney Joe a cherry and a sweet kiss, Billy Britt a cherry and a sweet kiss, and ate the other cherries herself.

"*Dosvidanya*," she said, and picking up her practice bag, left the nice boys and walked out of the bar as though tiptoeing gracefully on eggs.

The stagehands had begun to move the scenery for *Giselle* into place, but Emma and Freddie were still rehearsing the Ashton pas de deux they were doing the next night. She had always driven Freddie; this season, she was driving him like a Fury, rehearsing at odd hours like this because there was so little time or space on the schedule for them. She was determined to achieve a performance he simply wasn't capable of anymore. Nor was she, but she wouldn't admit it.

To Freddie, she seemed totally unaware they were prancing in front of scenery for a ballet they'd been heaved out of and would never dance again. Christ, the theater could go up in flames and she wouldn't know it, wouldn't quit rehearsing. Wouldn't quit, period. Well, that was part of what made her extraordinary.

He liked working with her and was fond of her, although it made him physically uncomfortable, more so after all the years, to see the terrifying pleasure she got from performing. Her best orgasms, he suspected, came from her best performances. Well, there were those who thought he and Annabelle were kinky, and he was among them. What the hell: all the characters in and around ballet were kinky, one way or another. At least Emma's kinkiness paid off. A good thing, too, because she was his bread and butter. Not much bread next year: they'd be doing one-nighters in Bridgeport and Dayton and St. Paul, high-school auditoriums. Christ. Annabelle had to stop spending as though Emma and he had a future.

At the edge of the wings, Sevilla and Yuri, in their first-act *Giselle* costumes, were ready for a final brief warm-up as soon as Emma and Freddie got off the stage. Sevilla lit a fresh cigarette while Yuri massaged the knot between her shoulders.

"You know why Adelaide butters me up?" Sevilla asked rhetorically.

"Why we don't butter each other up?" Yuri automatically kissed the back of her neck.

"You're revolting." She fitted the cigarette into her long holder. "She knows I want to dance in Milan and Rio, but she's determined to get me to do her bloody tour again."

"Why you don't say no?"

"You're exactly like Richard. He says I've gotten pathological about saying no to anyone who asks me to dance nowadays."

"Who is Richard?" Yuri asked, not really caring.

"Richard, Yuri my love"—Sevilla lowered her voice—"is why I am not going to end up like

Emma." She saw Emma and Freddie coming toward them. "Oh, right there!" she said loudly to Yuri, wriggling her shoulders.

"I've got a marvelous man for that, Sevilla." Emma wiped her face with a towel.

"No injections. I faint at the sight of a needle."

"No, no, just massage. I'll leave his number in your dressing room."

"You're an angel, Emma," Sevilla said, and kissed Emma, making herself feel much less guilty.

Emma hadn't overheard, but she recognized fear when she saw it. She saw it often enough in her mirror. Sevilla, she figured, had about five more years. She didn't begrudge them; besides, Sevilla, good as she undoubtedly was, had never been and never would be what Emma was. Still was.

She walked down the corridor to her dressing room, her arm around Freddie to make up to him for what she had put him through and would continue to put him through. At the far end, the elevator to the dressing rooms on the other floors opened, and dancers came out in costume, ready for Act One. Lovely, lost Giselle. Emma gasped.

"Oh, God!" She let go of Freddie and started racing down the corridor.

Emilia was sitting on the floor of the empty elevator in street clothes. She smiled at Emma's startled face and waved a boozy hello as the elevator doors shut and she was carried up and away.

Emma wasn't amused. She was angry. She started back to her dressing room, regretting the time wasted in developing Emilia into an extension of her own life. It wasn't a question of dedication, but of professionalism. She had always had little patience with anyone who wasn't professional, less with drunks, with anyone who lost control. Oh, it was hard to hang on sometimes; nobody knew that better than she, particularly these days. But what was the point of letting a carefully built-up facade shatter? Why howl your pain out loud? Who cared? Nobody could do anything about it but yourself; it wouldn't bring anyone closer. The reverse, really.

The closest she'd come to breaking through her facade and exposing herself was to Deedee, the other afternoon at Dahkarova's. Even then, she'd stopped short of saying how badly she hurt. She'd wanted to let go and cry and have Deedee put her arms around her; fortunately, the habit of control was too strong. True, Deedee cared, she was all sympathy. Underneath, however, if she wasn't pleased, she was at least comforted to discover Emma's life wasn't that much more satisfactory now than her own. And therefore thought less of Emma. Understandable: misery loves company. That's the way people were, and that was why letting go led only to mutual self-pity.

That, she had learned from her mother. At twelve, when her father left, she started to build her facade; at seventeen, she was totally professional. Perhaps rigidly so; perhaps that was what was wrong with her life. No, what was wrong was inevitable: age and decay, which confronted everyone sooner or later. But other people slipped casually into decline without ever having seen the view from the top. She had, and oh, God, it was magnificent! Something only the special few, the talented, could see. Emilia had that talent; Emilia was that good; she had to see that view, if she had to be dragged up there.

By the time Emma got to the girls' dressing room, Emilia had her clothes off. She was smiling dreamily into the mirror while Sandra struggled to put her into tights.

"What did she have?" Emma asked.

"Cherries," Sandra said.

"For remembrance," Emilia added in the Russian accent, and giggled.

The stage manager's voice came over the speaker, calling places. The curtain was going up.

"Can you cover for her in this act?"

"We're only in Act Two. Soloists," Sandra said grandly. "We lead the Wilis, and then—"

"I know," Emma interrupted, annoyed. "How are you going to get that off?" She pointed to Sandra's zipperless turtleneck; she was already in full makeup.

"Oh, shit!"

Emma grabbed a bathrobe for Emilia, and turning her head away from the too-sweet smell of liquor, led her out of the room.

"Bye-bye," Emilia called back to Sandra, who was cutting her turtleneck with a pair of scissors. It was easier to get a new one, and she had put on a particularly dazzling makeup.

There was a shower in Emma's dressing room. She let it run ice cold, shoved Emilia under, and slammed the door. She didn't know how long was safe; she didn't know how to handle a drunk. When she let Emilia out, the girl was gasping and frozen. Emma wrapped her in a big towel.

"Thank you. I'm fine now."

"Really?"

"Oh, yes. That was good," Emilia said, and smiled: she felt lovely and light-headed and gay. "What a nice dressing room! And what a nice towel!"

Emma eyed her suspiciously. "Are you still drunk?"

"No."

"I can say you're sick."

Through a furry haze, Emilia realized Emma wanted her to go on. It was important to Emma that she go on, and she wanted very much to please Emma. "I'm not sick. I'm not exactly sober, but I'm fine."

She did seem fine as Emma watched her from the wings. She was dancing a little behind

the music, but not too much, she'd get by.
Then she began to smile. Any smile was out of
place on the spirit of a dead virgin in a ceme-
tery, but this was a boozy smile. Sandra, dancing opposite Emilia, caught it out of the corner
of her eye and tried to kill it with a muted
glare. Emilia winked, turned to the wings, and
seeing Emma's look of concern, incorporated a
little reassuring hand wave into the choreography. And smiled even more broadly when, to
her surprise, she found herself doing a smooth
bourrée right into the wings. Emma reached
out to push her gently back out onstage. Emilia
smiled her gratitude.

Out front, where Deedee stood along the
wall, one of the dancers watching with her
smothered a giggle.

"Rinky-dink zonkerooed," he muttered to his
friend.

"What?" Deedee asked.

The man sitting on the aisle told them to be
quiet.

Deedee's cheeks were burning, but because
of Emilia. Something was very wrong: she
looked like a badly dubbed movie where the
mouth kept moving after the voice had
stopped. When Sandra and the others stopped,
Emilia moved; when they went up, she went
down; when they went left, she went right,
changed her mind, went left, and bumped
smack into Sandra.

"Zonker-reeny-rooed!" The kid was really laughing now.

Suddenly Emilia's smile was replaced by a sick look. Her hands fluttered to her stomach for an instant; she began breathing hard; her eyes darted to the wings in panic. Deedee pushed her way out of the auditorium, ran down the corridor to the pass door to backstage, and scurried through.

She got to the edge of the wings to find Emma yanking handfuls of Kleenex from the box on a light stand. Emilia came off, and Emma put one arm around her and hurried her to a far corner where there was a fire bucket. Helplessly, Deedee stood and listened to the muffled sound of retching. At least Emilia had held out until her proper exit, for Sandra was in the wings, nervously getting more Kleenex ready.

At last the pathetic sound stopped. Deedee opened her bag, took out a handkerchief. Emilia came out of the darkness, her makeup chalk, her pale body greasy with sweat. Deedee took a step toward her, holding out her hands. Emilia looked at her and through her and turned away to let Emma take the Kleenex from Sandra and mop her damp face. Emma didn't seem to know Deedee was even there. She was too concerned, too concentrated on drying Emilia, on getting her back onstage, on willing her to get through the rest of the performance. Sober now, Emilia was ashamed, but not miserable anymore, not in pain, not even sad. That had to be because Emma was standing in the wings to help her, and would remain in the wings to help her. Emma, unlike her mother, really cared.

For Emma, home was a midtown building that had been a convenient hotel for her, then became an apartment hotel, and was now a co-op with a switchboard, maid service, and a small restaurant left over from the original regime. Everything in the three rooms was hers, careful purchases or thoughtful gifts: the antique furniture with pale silk upholstery; the delicately framed photographs and paintings, mostly of herself, on the pastel walls; the needlepoint pillows (mainly her work); the porcelain figurines of dancers, the collection of crystal swans, the miniature musicians made of gold, the beaded flowers. It was the only home she had. She had lived there for years, yet it seemed as temporary as her dressing room.

Emilia, lying on the sofa in one of Emma's silk-and-lace nightgowns, covered by the softest blanket, her head on one of Emma's pillows, thought the apartment was as beautiful, as perfect, as Emma's diamond earrings. It had been stupid to get drunk, but lucky to get sick and brought home to this watercolor palace and be fed soup and tea and biscuits in thin, translucent dishes that Emma was now clearing from the rosewood coffee table to the little kitchenette behind the hand-painted screen. She was still hungry, but it would be insensitive to say so.

Emma had listened to the saga of Emilia and Yuri and Carolyn without comment. She hadn't known what to say. She didn't know how to deal with Emilia's openness: whether to treat her as a child, protégée, colleague, friend, person, what? At Emilia's age, Emma had been a young woman: facade constructed, road mapped, destination set. But snuggling on the sofa was a little girl—at least, that was what those enormous sea-blue eyes seemed to belong to most of the time. But other times, the sea changed, turned winter blue, and the girl had an odd sophistication that made Emma feel inexperienced, incapable. As when Emilia brusquely dismissed Deedee, coldly brushed aside any mention of her, yet seemed to be pulling advice from Emma as though she were her mother.

It rattled Emma. She didn't know how to be a mother, didn't want to be anyone's mother. Yet she liked having this girl here, liked taking care of her, wanted to take care of her, to help her. The unfamiliar feeling took her by surprise. Inexplicably, she no longer felt Emilia had to become Emma. She wanted her to, wished she would; would do anything and everything to help; but maybe the girl wanted something more. Or less. Whichever, Emma would not push; at least, she would try not to.

Nevertheless, the only subject she could talk about with security was dancing, which could be construed as pushing, even though she was merely answering Emilia's eager questions.

"Oh, yes, the right partner is absolutely essential," Emma said. "And Michael was very good for me."

"What happened?"

"He became a choreographer." That wasn't the whole truth. She tried to behave like Deedee. "Shouldn't you go to sleep?"

"Oh, not yet." Emilia certainly did not want a mother, she wanted a friend. "I meant what happened with you and Michael?"

"Priorities." Another evasion, which Emilia misinterpreted.

"Oh. He liked boys better than girls."

"Not then." Emma laughed, embarrassed. "Well, how do I know? We didn't talk quite so openly in those days." The subject made her uncomfortable. She picked up one of her little dogs, and told the blunt truth. "Michael knew my priority was dancing."

"Are you sorry?"

"I don't believe in ever being sorry," Emma said flatly. "We are what we are."

"Am I like you?"

It was so tempting to give the wanted answer, but she didn't. "Oh, Emilia, darling, I don't know." Another of the little dogs was yapping jealously. Emma picked him up. "Are you sure you don't want to call home?"

"I'd only wake Ethan. Emma, I've stayed at Yuri's a lot."

Which was she? A little girl saying her mother was having an affair that upset her, or a young woman illustrating her experience? Emma was bewildered. "You continually surprise me."

"And me!" Emilia agreed delightedly. "I wish I knew what I was."

"You will."

"When?"

"Oh, something happens." Emma began to turn out the lamps. "There's always a moment ... Perhaps when Yuri wants to come back."

"I don't want him back," Emilia said coolly. "Of course, I'd love to dance with him. I liked going to bed with him, but I wanted it to be more. And that gets in the way, doesn't it?"

It did, Emma remembered. "Which do you want the most?" She looked at Emilia's face and laughed. "Both!" She turned out a lamp by the sofa. "Well, that's something to dream about. Good night."

"Good night."

The little dogs scampered after Emma as she crossed the darkened living room to the bedroom door.

"Emma ... it's so nice here."

"I'm glad," Emma whispered.

She took her sleeping pill and went to bed, feeling happier than she had in a very long time.

The next morning, Emma stopped by the American Ballet office, presumably to pick up her check.

"Is Adelaide busy or really busy?" she asked the secretary.

"Your guess is as good as mine. She and Michael are figuring out the program for the Gala."

Gala performances were originally given on an anniversary to raise money for the company. Now that they were an annual event, they had become a series of dazzling vaudeville-like turns, demanding an ever bigger roster of stars, and hopefully, one novelty or surprise. Each year, the Gala made Emma more nervous: the other ballerinas got younger and more international. However, she had a mission. She knocked on the door and barged in.

Adelaide and Michael were seated at her big desk in the middle of a jumble of scarred antiques and Salvation Army treasures.

"Look at that, dearie!" Adelaide held out an old poster. "Our very first Gala."

Emma read the names. "You were still dancing then. So were you, Michael."

"And you were in the corps de ballet," he said.

They looked at each other fondly, remembering.

"Cinderella watching all the stars go to the fancy party afterward," Emma said.

"But then we went to that little bar across from the old Met and had our party."

And after that, she and Michael had gone to his walk-up in the Village for the first time. Emma handed back the poster. "Galas are worse than the Olympics."

"Dearie, you're not nervous after all these years?"

"Of course not." Emma smiled sweetly. "I'm only going to be competing against the greatest dancers you two can snare in your net."

"But you mustn't think of it as a competition," Adelaide said.

"No," Michael said. "Just think of the two hundred and fifty tax-deductible dollars a seat we're going to charge."

"And get. Oh, dearie, this is going to be a gala gala! Marcia and Richard are coming from Stuttgart, Anthony and Lynn from London . . ." She turned to Michael. "You don't suppose they'd travel tourist?"

"No, Adelaide."

Emma realized there was no way of maneuvering the conversation, she'd have to plunge in. "I hear you're doing a section from Arnold's ballet at the Gala."

"Well, it's different . . . and novel, and . . ."

Emma watched Adelaide's hands flutter, let her founder in discomfort a moment. It would help. "Oh, I think it might be rather exciting," she offered.

"Exactly what we thought!" Adelaide was ecstatic with relief.

"Then Emilia should really be invited to the party after," Emma said casually. Michael began to laugh. "And Arnold, of course."

"Oh. So they should," Adelaide said a bit reluctantly.

"And so they will." Michael was really laughing now. He bowed to Emma. "Bravo."

"Brav*a*," she corrected, and curtsied. "And *merci*—to you both."

She waltzed out, gaily triumphant: she'd already arranged to meet Emilia during her lunch hour at the dressmaker who did her own clothes. He was another of the tall, tanned young men in jumpsuits who would soon be ten times as expensive. Then his boutique would become a salon, he would take over his building, a conglomerate would take him over, and together they would put out a new perfume and his complete line of monogrammed everything.

His untidy fitting room had a multipaneled mirror in which Emilia could see herself from almost every angle. The dress Emma had chosen for her would never be out of fashion. Each of Emma's dresses was kept in its own plastic bag, occasionally shortened or lengthened, but never discarded. They never had to be.

"It's too big and too long," she said to the designer. "It should be a size four."

"It will be when we're through." He gave additional instructions to the fitter. "When's the Gala?"

"Tuesday next."

"We could have it a size three by then. Turn around, lovey," he said to Emilia.

She obeyed, examining herself in all the mirrors. "It looks like a nightgown," she announced.

The designer turned to Emma. "Do you want to hit her, or shall I?"

In the box, the dress looked expensive; on the hanger, it looked beautiful. Emilia ran her hand down it lovingly, then carefully hung it in the closet.

"It's very pretty," Deedee said unenthusiastically. She gathered up the tissue paper on Emilia's bed and crumpled it as though it were Emma. In the remembered picture of the reflected images in the mirrored wall, Emma moved in front of her, cut her out. Which, she saw now, was really what had happened. She threw the crumpled tissue into the wastebasket.

Emilia closed the closet door. "Why are you angry?" She might have been asking Deedee why she was standing.

"Why are you?" Deedee snapped.

"I'm not."

"You damn well are. You just cover it up with ice. Like Emma."

Emilia calmly began putting the dress box back together.

"That horny little Russian behaved like a bastard, so you take it out on me," Deedee said. "I didn't hide anything from you. I brought Rosie here. You knew what was—"

"I have to wash my hair." She opened the door to the bathroom, but Deedee slammed it shut.

"You sit down and listen to me!"

Dutifully Emilia sat on the edge of her bed, folded her hands in her lap.

"When Daddy and Janina come, you want them to see us like this? You want to hurt them, too? Let's talk it out—"

"There's nothing to talk out."

"Stop punishing me!" She hated her anger, hated her voice, hoped Ethan couldn't hear, that he was watching television. She sat next to Emilia and took one of her hands in both of hers. Surely she would understand, she wasn't a little girl anymore.

"Daddy and I have loved each other for twenty years. That's a long time. It isn't the same now. We love each other, it's good, but ... it's different. After twenty years, you get to need, to want a little something, a little ... Emilia, look at me? Please look at me. Daddy and I have been away from each other all summer. I miss him. But sometimes when you miss someone—"

"Daddy wouldn't do what you did."

"How do you know?"

"I know Daddy."

"Like you know Yuri! I'm the only louse! Come on, Emilia, be fair!" She was crying now, but she didn't give a damn. "O.K., you hurt. I understand, I can help. Let me. Don't shut me out, we're friends. Nobody can help you better than I can! Nobody understands you better than I do, nobody!"

"Oh, Mama . . ."

She couldn't understand why Emilia sounded so sad. "What? What?"

Emilia got up. "You're really just angry about Emma, aren't you?"

"No." She couldn't stand the way the girl was looking at her. "No! I love you!" The words came in a burst as she jumped up and took Emilia in her arms and tightly held her to her. It was like holding stiff cardboard.

Chapter Eight

The moment she arrived at the theater and saw the size of the crowd, Adelaide forgot she was aching with fatigue. Dressed in a ruffled taffeta evening gown (she had forgotten she had bought a new summery one until she was in her limousine), she planted herself in the bulging lobby next to the sandwich board for the Gala with its streamer screaming SOLD OUT. Each time she spotted a board member of a foundation or someone who had made or could make a hefty contribution, she waved her souvenir program and her gloves like semaphore flags, pointing to the streamer and to the ceiling. Upstairs on the mezzanine was where the party was being held after the performance. Tax-deductible, a table at the party cost more than the best seats for the performance.

The usual glitterati swarming into the theater delighted her, but she regarded their dress as less than thrilling. Black tie and bejeweled evening gowns, yes; seersucker suits and long cotton dresses—passable, for the balconies. But the jacketless hordes in ostentatiously faded denims and flowered shirts, gaping with arrows of nudity pointing to bisexual crotches—no, terrible; never. And a vulgar lie, because many of them, too many, were holding orchestra tickets.

Audiences should look as splendid as the theater they were going to, dammit; their dress should reflect what they were going to see. A gala performance was an Event; the ballet itself was an art that deserved and demanded elegance.

But elegance was long gone from the world. As was her husband, the most truly elegant man she had ever known. Ames used to say ballet was for the elite, and accused her of wanting her audiences to look elite. She missed him badly these days, but he was wrong. Ballet was for everybody: one reason she still insisted on lots of popular-priced seats. Not that those denimed slobs sat there. They spent as much money and more time choosing their meticulously tailored, boutique-made rags than she had on the gown she had forgotten to wear. Or as Michael and Peter, standing with her, had on their clothes: Michael in his handsome black velvet dinner jacket, Peter in his too-sexual black silk jumpsuit with a heavy silver belt leering just above his groin. Yes, the jumpsuit had a certain style; but real style, like elegance, was something he was too young to have known. Even ballerinas, barring those of the old school like Emma, no longer had style offstage. Or elegance.

Oh, it was once so exciting merely to walk into a theater! Everyone, really everyone, looked so beautiful that romance was possible. These days, it was impossible, nonexistent, and therefore laughed at, called camp. Sex was presumably the substitute, but it had been made ordinary even when freakish. Like the get-ups that were freakishly ordinary. At least, if they were genuinely bizarre ... They weren't, though. The bizarre was gone, too. Along with candlelight and conversation and manners. And her money, if she was really going to make a list. All that remained of so much she had loved was ballet, currently riding the crest, but soon, she suspected, to slip down the money hill again, and perhaps permanently. Ah, but one thing did remain: her stubbornness. She would sell tickets to anyone in anything—loincloths, leaves, caked mud—if it gave her that streamer across the signboard for her Gala: SOLD OUT.

"Now, if we sell out the last two weeks," she burbled triumphantly to Michael and Peter, "we end the season with a deficit of less than eighty thousand!"

"Imagine," Michael said.

"About the price of your necklace," Peter added.

Adelaide laughed. "Oh, dearie, this is paste.

The real one went ... What did it go for, Michael?"

"The musicians' strike."

"Oh, yes. Pigs." Ames would have laughed and called that an elitist remark. But everyone, even the stagehands who spent half the evening playing poker in the basement, had higher minimums than her dancers. Pigs, they were; and old pigs, most of them, outlasting the dancers, outlasting everyone but her.

"Shouldn't we go backstage?" Michael asked.

"I'm not up to it." All that nervousness and temperament? No, thank you. She dispatched Peter to dispense verbal Valium and kisses. She'd wear out her mouth congratulating them afterward. There was nothing she could do now; the performance was in their hands.

Backstage, they knew it was, and the knowledge made them nervous. More nervous because it was a Gala, and, as Emma had said, a Gala was a three-ring competitive circus. They could hear the orchestra tuning away, and busied themselves warming up, refining their makeup, testing pointe shoes, checking costumes, counting flowers. Huge bouquets from the management, fans, friends, parents, lovers, mates—some even *to* themselves *from* themselves—crammed the dressing rooms, overflowed into the corridors, making passage difficult and dangerous.

Carter had sent Emma a diamond clip instead of flowers, then had changed his mind and sent a very grand bouquet as well. To make sure she kept her status onstage, she guessed. The clip was wrong for the new dress hanging on the wall. She would wear the diamond earrings, no other jewelry. She put the clip away and continued her rituals.

She had warmed up early; had made Freddie put an Ace bandage around his bad knee ("I promise you it doesn't show through those tights"), had made up slowly, combed out her wig herself, repaired a tiny rent in her costume, and sewn new ribbons on her shoes. Now she sat at the dressing table, staring at herself in the mirror, ready to become a Russian, ready to concentrate on transforming controlled Emma into passionate Anna.

There was a knock. Emilia came in, leg warmers and a sweater over her costume. Emma had supervised her makeup.

"Nervous?"

Emilia shook her head. "I'm concentrating, like you told me."

"*Merde.*" Emma kissed her for luck.

"*Merde.*" Emilia returned the kiss, but delayed leaving. "Well, Arnold wants me onstage."

"Don't let him change anything," Emma warned.

"I won't." She turned to go, still hesitant. "Will you watch from the wings?"

"Yes. But you won't see me."

"Thank you. For everything. And I'll watch

you, but you'll be wonderful. *Merde*." She kissed Emma again and went quickly down the corridor.

Emma almost followed, wanted to say something more, something to reassure, to encourage, to tell her stage fright was normal. But it wasn't normal for Emma, and she had it, must be having it. Otherwise, why was she preparing now for a five-minute excerpt from a ballet she had done hundreds of times, and wasn't going to do for at least an hour? Back to the rituals. She shook her hands briskly, then took deep breaths—slow in, slow out, in slowly, out slowly, relax in, relax out.

Ironically, there was too much time. She couldn't sit. She would visit her co-stars from abroad and wish them luck. She looked at herself in the mirror: yes, she was going to give a gala performance tonight. She was going to be extraordinary.

In a corner of the stage, Carolyn, her spangled Black Swan costume glittering like her tiara, practiced *fouettés* in plastic leg warmers, still undecided about shoes for the party. If she wore the silver, she would dwarf Yuri and look like a white ostrich, particularly with all those feathers. On the other hand, if she wore the Capezio slippers, she'd trip over the dress unless she held it up. And that would ruin the line. Maybe he was going to wear his boots with really high heels. She'd find out and then decide. Her *fouettés* were absolute perfection.

In another corner, Yuri kept stretching his legs, trying not to listen to Sevilla, who was making him nervous. He kept stretching, she kept talking, not making a move to warm up.

"And then the bastard said"—she was smoking, of course—"'Sevilla, if you don't cancel Australia, we're finished.' Well, you know me. I got right out of bed and said, 'Richard, I never cancel. You're finished.' Oh, Yuri, what do I do now?" she wailed.

"For God's sake, Sevilla," he said irritably, "just try to dance well."

She looked at him in astonishment. "Oh, darling, I will."

She would, too. A delicate Meissen doll, she had no nerves. Which made him more irritable. He released his tension in an incredibly fast line of turns, ending upstage, where Arnold was giving Emilia last-minute corrections.

"You are making her nervous," Yuri said.

"I'm not nervous." Emilia blushed.

"I am not either." Happy because of his clean, fast turns, Yuri began to clown, shaking with exaggerated fear. "Why should I be? Is only biggest night of season, is only your biggest opportunity, Arnold's biggest opportuni—"

"Just shut up," Arnold cut in. He wanted to tell him to go back to Russia, but Arnold's father was practically a charter member of the ILGWU and an old-time Marxist. Besides, Yuri was hands-down brilliant; maybe someday he'd dance in one of Arnold's ballets. If he got the chance to do another ballet after tonight. His stomach shot the chutes again, and he ran for the nearest john.

"Is all right to be nervous," Yuri said to Emilia.

She didn't answer.

"Me, I am always nervous until I hit stage. Then . . . all gone." He smiled.

She still didn't answer.

"*Merde*, Emilia," he said softly, and kissed her on the lips.

"*Merde*," she replied as coldly as possible, tightening her lips because she wanted so badly to kiss him back. He waited. She prayed she could stand there and let him wait a long, long time. If she did, he might laugh and walk away. If he did, she could kick him in the behind. That was another traditional way of wishing luck. He could take it any way he wanted. He had a beautiful behind. Another tradition was to grab someone in the crotch, but she couldn't dare do that. She wished he would go away, not stand there looking at her the way he did when they made love.

She kissed him. His hands came up to cradle her face, but before he could touch her, she made herself walk away. Concentration, Emma had said over and over; concentration made a performance.

She was heading from the stage to the

dressing rooms when she caught a flash of orange and brown in the wings. Smoothly she switched direction and came downstage where she stood, shaking her hands and breathing in and out as Emma had taught her.

The orange and brown was the same chiffon print Deedee had worn when the ballet came to the Music Hall in Oklahoma City. Only her evening bag, hanging limply from her wrist by a thin gold-looking chain, was new. Inside was an opening-night present for Emilia—a little real gold heart. Corny, maybe, but God knows symbolic. She was skulking in the wings, waiting to give Emilia her heart, when she saw Emilia deliberately turn to duck her. As though she was Rose, that monster stage mother in *Gypsy*. Some of the smart-ass dancers referred to her as Rose; she'd heard them. Untrue, unfair, plain bitchy, but preferable to what she got from Emilia.

They slept in the same room, sat at the same table, shared the same bathroom, and Emilia was as contained, courteous, and respectful as though she was Lizzie Borden (in the De Mille ballet) and was counting on Ethan and Dahkarova to be witnesses in her favor. Her politeness cut so deep that Deedee wanted to scream or cry or slap her. Instead, she grew a leaden lump of pain in the belly where she had carried this child who now hated her. No: didn't hate her, was disgusted with her, angry with her; she'd get over it.

But when? Ballet classes in Oklahoma ended Saturday, and Wayne would arrive with Janina on Sunday. He had wanted to fly up for the Gala and back the next morning. Luckily, the insane airline schedules were in conspiracy with her, and she'd managed to con Wayne into waiting to see Emilia in the completed ballet. Whenever that was. She'd implied next week, but it might be next season. She was just stalling desperately, of course. If Wayne walked in now, he'd see the deep freeze in one minute flat; and in five, Deedee would be telling him the cause, she'd have to. But that poor damn fool idiot child of hers was the one who would suffer. Because as much as Wayne loved Emilia, he loved Deedee more. That was something Emilia didn't understand, something Deedee had hoped and still hoped Emilia would never have to understand. Yuri should have done it, should have made her a young woman, but he hadn't. The little prick had turned her into an ice maiden, even colder than Emma, and that was no way to live.

Deedee walked decisively out on the stage: let them call her Rose! Emilia, doing that silly deep breathing, was such a baby. Surely the excitement of a first Gala would make anyone approachable, even vulnerable and eager for support. Not Emilia, apparently. Deedee clutched her new bag, felt the outline of the little box with the gold heart, tried to smile and talk, but the words couldn't get past the lump in her throat. Her eyes brimming, she held up two crossed fingers for luck.

Emilia mirrored the gesture, holding up her crossed fingers longer than she had to. Deedee could see the child's hesitancy, her confused conflict. She knew she shouldn't move closer, but she did. Emilia quickly brushed her cheek with her lips and spun into a circle of turns that took her far away.

Be grateful for the smallest of favors from disapproving children. Deedee mustered up a smile, and as she walked down the dressing-room corridor, decided to leave Emilia's present on her dressing table.

"Don't you look nice!" It was Emma, standing in her doorway.

Nice. In a dress that Emma, who was so fussy about clothes, didn't remember. Nice. In a dress that was fine for Oklahoma City, frumpy for New York. Behind Emma, she could see the *Anna Karenina* costume on a hanger. There was a pair of scissors on the table. She had to restrain herself.

"You're doing *Anna*." She followed Emma into the dressing room.

"The suicide scene," Emma said gaily. She lifted her wig off its block. "All the other ladies are going to wear short tutus and do at least one hundred pirouettes, so this not-so-young lady is going to be covered to the floor and act up a storm."

Deedee traced the costume with one finger,

[179]

then held out the skirt of the incredible evening gown hanging next to it. "This is really a knockout."

"Want to be my date for the party?" Emma put the wig on, beginning to become Anna. "Or do you have one?"

"No. That's kaput." The scene with Rosie had been very painful (he'd gotten angry enough to make a crack about Wayne's ballet bisexuality), but that was none of Emma-Anna's business. Nor was Emilia, and let her get *that* message. "Listen, Emma, that's a terrific dress you gave Emilia, but you shouldn't have."

"She's my godchild, why not?"

"You just shouldn't have." Deedee's voice shook. "*Merde.*" She kissed Emma quickly and went out.

She took the elevator to Emilia's floor, hurrying to get to her dressing room and leave the present next to her makeup before she got there. There was no card. With an eyebrow pencil, she managed on a piece of Kleenex: "I love you, Mother." The point broke. In the old days, Emma would have killed her for using the pencil. And did, in that mirrored wall. And was doing it again. Better to forget her; better still to have a drink. But over the loudspeaker, she heard applause and music. The performance had begun.

She hugged the wall close to an exit door, thinking she'd spend most of the evening in the bar. Certainly her feet would hurt in these damn shoes that still didn't fit right. Almost immediately, however, the beauty of what she was seeing pulled her out of herself. She lost consciousness of everything but the splendor on the stage. It was dazzling, thrilling, as magical as she had thought a million *barres* ago. And she was part of it; even only as a teacher of beginners, she was part of this family, this world of artists. She stayed against the wall, pleased and proud that standing there marked her as one who belonged.

Then the curtain went up on Emma as Anna Karenina, and Deedee was an ex-dancer who had a ballet school in the provinces, a summer teacher, nobody. It was unbearable to look at what she might have been. She pushed open the exit door and stumbled into the corridor, her whole body trembling so badly she had to brace herself against the wall with both hands. She needed Wayne.

She pressed hard, breathing carefully. The trembling subsided, stopped. Now she really did need a drink. As she started across the thick red carpet, another door opened, and Michael came out of the auditorium. He closed the door very carefully, muffling the music, then saw Deedee and shrugged.

"I can't watch it anymore," he said quietly. "They're too old for it, and that depresses me. I'm too old, too used up to do another, and that depresses me even more."

"It's a beautiful ballet, Michael." Deedee patted his hand, giving him the comfort she wanted. "It'll last forever."

"Why can't we?" He looked at her curiously. "Why aren't you watching?"

She shrugged. "It hurts. I keep seeing Emma and me rehearsing for you . . . Hey, will you tell me something? Truthfully?"

"What?"

"Oh, Jesus. Can you believe I've wanted to ask this for about twenty years?" She faked a laugh. "O.K. . . . Michael, if I hadn't been pregnant, would you have used me as Anna instead of Emma?"

He rummaged in the past: he'd been scared his ballet would fail. But even that terror was under a layer of mist. And Deedee? "I don't remember. I honestly don't, Deedee."

People remembered what had been important to *them*. "I wish to hell I didn't," she said.

They stood quietly, staring down the corridor of their different memories. At the far end, the door leading backstage opened and Arnold came tearing through just as Michael had done twenty years ago in another theater for another ballet.

"Oh, God!" Deedee pulled Michael after her into the auditorium.

They were still cheering Emma. Another bow, and another. Deedee found Arnold against the wall, gripped his hand. Emma's bows added to their nervousness. Then, at last, quiet. The conductor raised his baton, the music began, and there was her daughter, alone on the huge stage.

Later, she realized she had seen only thirty seconds before she had gone deaf and blind with tears. But Emilia must have been good, because there she was, smiling and bowing to the racketing audience, getting flowers, and there was frenetic Arnold running on from the wings. How did he get there so fast? The ballet must have scored, too, Arnold taking one bow, then another, the greedy son of a bitch, why didn't he bring Emilia forward? At least take her hand, bow to her. But then Arnold did just that, and Deedee heard herself cry "Bravo!"

To celebrate, Deedee had herself a small vodka at one of the little mezzanine bars. She would neither be missed nor satisfied backstage, that she knew. So while waiting for the main events to arrive at the party, she had herself another small vodka and wondered where she would sit.

The broad, high-ceilinged mezzanine with its skyscraper windows overlooking the plaza and its cool, vanilla marble floor had been swiftly set up for the champagne supper dance. Apple-green-and-white-striped tablecloths, centerpieces of honey-yellow flowers: very summer. Deedee, of course, was in autumn colors. What the hell: everyone was so rich, maybe they'd think it was deliberate. She was the only woman in the room who wasn't dripping a single jewel, but maybe they'd think that was deliberate, too. Understated elegance, ha-ha. The jaunty dance band in its leafy bower played tunes that were so old they were the latest fashion. The black ties and evening gowns chattered and laughed softly and smelled good; drank champagne at the round tables, talked-danced on the creamy stone floor; applauded the evening stars as flashbulbs popped. A good-taste party: Deedee felt more festive and more lonely.

Downstairs, the lobbyful of party watchers included middle- and lower-rank dancers from the company as well as the seersuckers, the peasant skirts, the artificially aged denims. The dancers were easy to spot: they all stood with their feet forming a V. At the bottom of the broad marble stairway leading up to the mezzanine, a green velvet rope was lifted only for those carrying the gilt-edged invitation cards.

Adelaide had no invitation, nor did Michael or Peter. For one wistful moment, Michael hoped the green barrier would not be lifted. He would have loved to see what Adelaide would do. But she was better known to the tuxedoed guards than all the glitter litter in the hall. They even bowed slightly as she and her escorts passed through.

A few feet on the wrong side of the velvet rope, Emilia waited in a daze for Arnold to say good night to some people. She knew she'd been onstage, she knew she'd put on the new dress, but she wasn't quite sure what had happened, where she was, who those people were with Arnold. Oh, yes—his parents, Mr. and Mrs. Berger.

The pear-shaped Bergers weren't old enough to have grown to look alike, they just did: proud fruit dumplings in dark blue. Arnold permitted his mother to kiss him for the tenth time, while his father pumped Emilia's hand over and over. Then, to his own surprise, too, Mr. Berger gallantly kissed Emilia's hand. Unlike Wayne physically, yet he was a Wayne, and she kissed him. Mrs. Berger hugged Mr. Berger with double delight, and they watched their young god and his goddess ascend to a heaven of fame, fortune, and grandchildren.

The partygoers applauded the entrance of Emilia and Arnold, but only one flashbulb flared, so Arnold led her out on the dance floor and whirled her close to the photographers. A great round of applause, even some cheers, and the photographers turned to focus on the landing at the top of the stairs: Yuri had arrived with Carolyn, her long, flowing dress lifted off the floor by a loop to one hand. She posed prettily, but Yuri made himself a mustache from her feather boa. Carolyn pretended to laugh: clowning because he was short, and because he was short, her dress was too long, and here he was, making her scurry after him like a silly date, across the dance floor to their table, where he had the nerve to stop and wink at Emilia who was dancing by! Winked because she scored so well tonight. Emilia didn't have the sense to wink back, poor girl. *She* was short enough for Yuri, and Yuri was not a partner to sneeze at.

From where Deedee sat at Adelaide's table, she couldn't see whether or not Emilia was wearing the little gold heart. When Peter had come to bring her to the table, she'd figured Emma had sent him. But Emma wasn't at the party yet. Probably going to make a grand entrance in that spectacular dress. So the summons must have come from Adelaide—which meant Emilia must have done damn well.

"To Emilia, dearie!" Adelaide raised her champagne, Michael and Peter raised theirs, Deedee raised her vodka.

"Tradition is continuity, and my God, I've lived to see it!" Adelaide's thin face glowed. "Second generation, in our family. And yours, of course." She patted Deedee's hand. "Now: what do we do with our baby ballerina?"

"Arnold's ballet?" Michael suggested.

"She doesn't do much more in the rest of it than she did tonight," Peter said.

"Well, the costumes are paid for, so we might as well do it," Adelaide said. "That ballet is going to help make the child a ballerina, and we're going to need a new one badly next year."

Deedee had to put her hands in her lap.

"She'd be lovely in *Sleeping Beauty*," Michael offered.

"Perfect," from Peter.

Deedee wondered if the two men hadn't plotted all this beforehand.

Adelaide put on her glasses and surveyed the other tables. "Who'll pay for the production? Well, someone. Particularly if we warm up Emilia this season in something with pizzazz that'll warm up the box office for next." She took off her glasses and turned to Deedee. "Want to tell her?"

"Nah," said Deedee, half out of her chair.

Joyfully she squeezed her way between the tables to get to Emilia on the dance floor. She was behaving like a crazy mother, but good news erases the past; the bearer is greeted with open arms and given her share of the present and the future.

Emilia wasn't wearing the heart. Exquisite in the new dress, she seemed encased in glass, unable to hear what Deedee was saying, unable to take it in. Maybe it was all too much for her.

"Well, isn't it wonderful? Aren't you excited?" Deedee urged.

"Yes," Emilia said vaguely, and turned to see who was being applauded now.

"You're going to be a ballerina! They're going to . . ." But the applause was drowning her out, warmly affectionate applause for an old favorite the room loved and wanted to show it still loved. Emma entered the room with

Freddie, her timing as perfect as her appearance.

Deedee was still, watching her daughter applaud, watching Emma come across the dance floor to them. Then Emma applauded Emilia and did a half-curtsy to her. The crowd loved it. So did the photographers. They pushed Deedee out of the way to get their pictures of the aging but beautiful ballerina paying graceful homage to the radiantly young and new, to the continuation of the line. Cold with rage, Deedee shoved through to the bar as Emma kissed Emilia, congratulated her, then slowly made her way with Freddie to Adelaide's table.

"Where's my bitch of a wife?" Freddie asked as they sat down.

"Now, dearie," Peter murmured.

"Very smart of you to do Anna," Adelaide said to Emma.

"Next time, she can lift me," Freddie complained. "I'm ready for traction."

"Worth it," Adelaide said. "Know what I'd like you to do for us next, Emma?"

Emma laughed happily and drank her champagne. "A new ballet!"

"Tradition makes a company."

"This is Adelaide's tradition night," Peter said.

"Shut up, Peter. I'd like to restore the full-length *Sleeping Beauty* to the repertoire."

"Oh, Adelaide!" Emma was very gay; the

evening couldn't have gone better. "Thank you, but I couldn't dance that anymore."

"No, but you could stage it."

The smile congealed on Emma's face. She managed to keep looking at Adelaide, to pick up her champagne, to take a sip, to put the glass back down, to listen politely and not scream.

"You know it inside out," Adelaide rattled on. "It could be fun, a new challenge. She'd do it beautifully, don't you think, Michael?"

"I think your timing is lousy, Adelaide."

Emma picked up her shimmering evening bag. "I must do something to my face."

When she was out of earshot, Adelaide said evenly, "Michael, even Emma has to move on. Like all the rest of us."

At the end of the little bar nearest the ladies' room, Deedee watched Emma coming, head high, regal ramrod posture. Apparently she was going to walk right by, so Deedee stepped forward and did a mocking imitation of Emma's half-curtsy. Emma's eyes were glazed. She put her bag on the bar and ordered champagne from the bartender. Her back was to the room, her profile to Deedee; she was somewhere else.

"Good evening, Emma."

"Good evening."

Deedee toyed with her vodka, then began, all lightness and charm. "Remember the fairy tales we used to take turns reading to Emilia? Like the one about the two princesses? Every time one opened her mouth, out came diamonds and rubies. Every time the other opened her mouth, out came newts and hoptoads. Newts and hoptoads"—she tapped her chest—"coming out."

"One of those little toads has already made an appearance."

"Really? When?"

"In my dressing room." Emma turned to her with an equally charming smile. "When you said I shouldn't have bought Emilia that dress. Twice, you said it. Just before a performance." She sipped her champagne. "I danced better tonight than I have in years."

"So I heard."

"Oh, another little toad. You've kept quite a few bottled up all these years, haven't you?"

"Ohhh ... embalmed, really."

"I think not. Why don't you let them out? I don't have a performance tomorrow." Emma signaled the bartender for a refill.

Deedee pushed her glass toward the man, came closer to Emma, and with a grin held out two clenched fists.

"O.K. Pick."

Emma looked amused. Gracefully she tapped Deedee's left fist. Deedee opened it and stared in mock surprise.

"Ah, a tiny one. I'd practically forgotten him." She leaned against the bar. "Why'd you make your best pal doubt herself and her hubby, Emma? Why'd you take the chance of lousing up her marriage? Why did you say, 'You better have that baby. It's the only way you can hold on to Wayne'? I'm just mildly curious now."

"You have a curious memory. But don't we all? As I remember, I said if you had an abortion, you might lose Wayne."

Deedee shook her head. "Sweet but inaccurate. I've remembered your exact words for lo these too many moons. I eventually figured out why you said 'em. Because you also said, 'Forget Michael's ballet, there'll be others.'" She laughed, wagging her finger. "You clever little twinkletoes. You knew a ballet like that comes once in a career. You wanted it real bad, so you lied to make sure you got what you wanted."

Smile for smile. "I've never had to lie to get what I wanted, Deedee. I'm too good."

"Really?"

"Oh, yes."

Deedee considered that. "Well, I suppose if you said 'bullshit,' you'd say it in French."

Even from the nearest table, they looked like two close friends enjoying a gossip, two very attractive women catching up and discovering a lot to laugh at merrily.

"If that word came as naturally to me as it does to you," Emma confided with more charm, "I'd have used it several times by now. In English. I think it more appropriate that you say it—to yourself. For trying to blame me for what you did. The choice was yours. It's much too late to regret it now, Deedee."

"And the same to you, Emma, me darlin'."

"I certainly don't regret mine." Enough was enough. Emma put down her glass and picked up her bag to leave.

"Then why are you trying to become a mother at your age?"

"Ohhh, that's not a little toad, that's a rather large bullfrog." Emma flipped her bag back on the bar. "I don't want to be anybody's mother. I think of Emilia as a friend. And one reason I tried to help—stupid me!—I thought it would make you happy if your daughter became what you wanted to be and couldn't be."

"Meaning you. It's so lovely to be you."

"Obviously you think so."

"Oh, no no no no no no!" Deedee trilled gaily up the scale, knowing she was getting to Emma.

"No no no no no?" An imitation.

"No. Alas. And I doubt if Emilia could become you. Oh, she's as talented. She works as hard. But there is one thing, dearest friend, that you are that she, poor darling, is not."

"And what, pray tell, is that?"

"A killer," Deedee said nicely. "You'll walk over anybody and still get a good night's sleep. That's what got you where you are, Emma."

She was smiling adorably. Emma smiled back, picked up her champagne, raised the glass—perhaps to take a sip, perhaps to make a toast—smiled again, and threw the champagne in Deedee's face. It was done so fast, anybody would have sworn it didn't happen. Even Deedee.

She felt the sharp splash, then the liquid dribbling down her face, down her chest, down her Oklahoma finery. "Good girl," she said, and picked up her bag and left.

But throwing the champagne had thrilled Emma like nothing before in her life. Grabbing her bag, she charged after Deedee, ignoring for the first time friends and admirers, thrusting aside hands held out to her. Spurred by the gunshot clatter of her heels, she raced down the marble stairway. Deedee was walking swiftly across the lobby.

"Deedee!" Emma yelled. "Deedee!"

She caught up with her as Deedee was pushing open the door to the plaza and grabbed her by the arm. "I'm sick to death of your jealousy and resentment!"

"So am I."

"Then stop blaming your goddamn life on me! You picked it!"

"You did," Deedee said angrily. "You took away the choice, you didn't give me the chance to find out if I was good enough."

"Well, I can tell you now: you weren't."

At that, Deedee broke away, pushed out into the plaza, and started walking rapidly across it toward the street. But Emma stormed after her, an uncontrollable hurricane of rage at everything.

"You knew yourself you weren't good enough," she shouted. "That's why you married Wayne!"

Deedee whirled around. "I loved him!"

"So much that you said to hell with your career?"

"Yes!"

"And got pregnant to prove you meant it?"

"Yes!"

"Lie to yourself, not to me." The toads tumbled out of Emma now. "You got married because you knew you were second-rate. You got pregnant because Wayne was a ballet dancer and that meant queer!"

"He wasn't!" Deedee said fiercely.

"Still afraid someone will think he is? You were terrified then. You had to prove to everyone he was a man. *That's* why you had a baby."

"That's a goddamn lie!"

"It's the goddamn truth!" Emma was shrieking like a fishwife and didn't give a damn, exulted in it, really. "You saddled him with a baby and blew his career. And now she's grown up and better than you ever were, and you're jealous!"

"You're certifiable. You'll use anything for an excuse."

"I'll use what for an excuse for what?"

"Trying to take away my child!"

Emma laughed. "I return the compliment: you're a liar!"

"And you're a user. You have been your whole life! Me, Michael—pretending to love him!—Adelaide, Freddie, and now Emilia."

"How Emilia?"

"'How Emilia!'" The locution maddened Deedee. "That display ten minutes ago: curtsy! applause! embrace! For *you*, not her! You were using her so everyone'd say: Emma's so gracious, Emma's so wonderful!"

"Untrue!"

But now Deedee was the fishwife. "You *are* wonderful! You're amazing! It's incredible how you keep going on. You're over the hill, you know it, and *you're* terrified. All you've got are your scrapbooks and your toe shoes and those stupid, fucking dogs! What are you going to fill in with, Emma? Not my daughter. You keep your goddamn hands off!"

"I'm a damn sight better for her than you are!"

"Like hell!"

"She came to me because her mother wasn't there. Her mother was too busy screwing her head off!"

"You bitch." That, Deedee didn't scream or shout. She said it low, and as she said it, slammed Emma with her evening bag. For a moment Emma was too shocked to move; but as she saw Deedee's arm start up again, she whacked at her with her own bag and tried to kick her in the ass at the same time. She missed on both counts, but Deedee thought the kick a good idea and tried to get in one of her own.

Behind them, the gargling fountains in the center of the plaza gave one last regurgitation, a little burp, and sputtered out. The floodlights shooting down from the three halls of culture went out. Only the silver summer moon and the spill of pale lemon rays from the party on the mezzanine were left to illuminate the two women in evening gowns flailing wildly at each other in the vast, empty square. Gasping, panting, fighting exhaustion as well as each other, they whacked and slammed and kicked, missing more often than not. They looked foolish, ridiculous: two middle-aged overdressed vaudevillians who didn't know how to get off. They had worn out their anger, they were just funny now. Deedee started to giggle first; that set Emma off, and soon they were both laughing and trying to get their wind back.

"Oh dear, oh dear," Deedee said. She took a few more breaths. "If there'd been a photographer handy, you'd have a whole new career."

"I must look awful." Emma opened her bag and took out her mirror.

"Nope: beautiful. I don't know how you do it."

Emma started to comb her hair. "Oh, I lost an earring."

"I'm sorry," Deedee was busy with her own comb.

"I'm not."

Deedee looked at her curiously. "Really?"

"Yes."

They began searching for the earring anyway. If they found it, fine; if they didn't, that was fine with Emma, too. The trappings weren't necessary anymore.

"Jealousy is poison," Deedee said. "Makes you a monster."

"Well, it does make one unfair." Then Emma grinned. "Two."

"Two?"

"Me, too."

Deedee laughed. "Oh, Emma, you made a good joke!"

"Yes, I did," Emma said proudly.

"Listen, you got off some really good ones before. Oh, look!"

It was the earring. She picked it up and gave it to Emma.

"Thank you. How did it get over here?"

"You also hit a couple of bull's-eyes before."

"So did you."

"Sit?"

"Oh, please."

Gratefully they sat on the rim of the quiet fountain. Faint dance music from the party floated over them, like nostalgia.

"I don't really remember what I said about having the baby," Emma said quietly. She swallowed a few times. "But I do know ... I would have said anything to make sure I got that ballet.... You were too good, Deedee, and I had to have it. I just had to."

It hadn't been such agony to say it, after all. She sat motionless, waiting.

"My God. Oh, Emma," Deedee said after a moment. Her eyes glistened, her voice cracked. "I didn't know how much I wanted you to say just that."

She put her arm around Emma's waist, and Emma put her arm around Deedee's waist. They sat like schoolgirls, listening to the melodies they had danced to so long ago.

"How's about a drink?" Deedee asked.

"Absolutely."

They stood up and began walking, their arms still around each other.

"It's good again," Emma said.

"You bet."

"I'm glad Wayne's coming."

"Me, too. ... How's with Carter?"

"*Ça va.*" Emma smiled. "*That's* 'bullshit' in French."

Deedee laughed. She had been heading for the street and a taxi, but Emma was leading her back to the party. She stopped and shook her head. "Not me."

"I have to." Emma pleaded for understanding. "This season, anyway."

How odd to feel that she, Deedee, was on

the top step. "Sure." She kissed her old friend. "Call me when you wake up."

"If not before!"

She watched Emma walk under the portico of the theater, watched her head go up, her back straighten elegantly. Her friend was a gallant lady. Upstairs, they would fuss over her, pour champagne for her, and she would smile and smile and smile. She was still a great ballerina, goddammit.

Emilia would come to her, and Emma would give her daughter advice on how to accomplish Adelaide's plans. Good advice. Better than she could give. And she had better get used to that. What she could give Emilia, Emilia didn't want. Maybe she would have to get used to that, too.

Chapter Nine

Two steps before he and Janina entered the arrival lounge at Kennedy, Wayne saw Deedee waiting, anxiety written all over her lovely face. It would be easy to erase that look. All he'd have to do was hear her confession and give her absolution. If she wanted to tell him what he'd pieced together anyhow from his phone call with Emilia, he could even make it easier for her. Wash it out by confessing how he, too, had fallen apart during the summer.

Naturally, there'd be initial awkwardness, but the kids would help them ride over that. He and Deedee would finally talk when they were going to bed, before they made love. He was nervous about that part. He wanted it to be really good, but was afraid it wouldn't be good enough. Even afraid it might not work.

Work. The word frightened him. Like most of the people he knew, Wayne was uncomfortable with words, yet was too often aware of the meaning below the surface of the first word that rose in his mind. Actually, he resented words: they fuzzed his meanings, everyone's. What they meant for you wasn't what they meant for someone else. On the other hand, he always knew clearly, instantly what someone else was thinking and feeling. Particularly someone he loved, like Deedee.

What was bothering him now was not the fling Deedee'd had during the summer—it never occurred to him that it might have been more than that—or her anxiety over it. He understood that; he could talk about that. No, what was truly bothering him, rumbling in his guts, was the restlessness in her that had prompted him to ship her off to New York City. Not the restlessness itself, but its cause, its real cause— which he *felt*, which he *knew* was he himself. Not just his homosexuality, but what he had done to her because of it.

That was a no-man's-land that had always lain between them, a danger zone he had always backed away from because it might be a mine field that could explode them. It had always troubled him, but in the beginning, when they got married, he had alibied: why spell it out? Honesty could be an overkiller. Anyway, trouble spots, like acne, disappeared as you got older. And they had; he'd relaxed. Until she began getting restless and he'd realized the cause wasn't just Oklahoma City. It was a frustration that was his fault.

Right then, he should have taken his own advice, the advice he had given her about Emma:

talk it out. But the damn words! Every one was a grenade that might blow up his no-man's-land and himself along with it. And then he would lose her, and he couldn't envision living, plain existence without her. What he should have done was tell her in the beginning. Over the years, a minor sore becomes a deadly infection that can erupt and kill the closeness between two people. Well, it had erupted in her restless frustration, and it could kill them. It would have been so much easier to tell her twenty years ago; he wished it were twenty years ago, and she had just told him she was pregnant.

He could have sworn Deedee was wishing exactly that now, in the airport lounge. He wanted to shout Yes! and explain and reassure, but a body thudded against his belly, Ethan was in his arms, and he caught a glimpse of Janina, her adolescent cool dropped like her tote bag as she ran to her mother and hugged her, a little girl again.

But where was Emilia? Why wasn't she there? He had let her down somehow; someone in the company had told her something ... No, stop, that was general damn-fool panic. But he looked at Deedee and suddenly sensed a connection between her anxiety and Emilia's absence. His family was splintering.

He managed to say hello and kiss Deedee over the heads of the two delirious kids, who kept holding on as though they would keep all of them together again and forever after. While they waited for the baggage, he kissed her again, still not a real kiss, but one meant to reassure her, along with the message in his eyes. But she wasn't reassured, and it did have something to do with Emilia, because she stumbled over her explanation of why Emilia wasn't there, and Ethan's interruptions didn't help.

"Wait a minute," Wayne said, and by simple questions managed to find out that even though it was Sunday, Emilia had spent the morning being coached by Emma and was being coached this afternoon by Dahkarova because she was dancing the *Don Quixote* pas de deux on Friday night.

"*Don Q!* You're kidding." It was a pas de deux Wayne had never danced. Even Deedee hadn't. It was reserved for ballerinas past, present, or hopefully, future.

"No, it's true," Deedee said, grateful Wayne was so impressed that he was sidetracked. "And you'll never guess who she's doing it with."

Wayne shook his head. "Oh, no!"

"Oh, yes. Yuri!"

"He'll wipe her out," Ethan predicted.

"Like hell he will!" Wayne said.

Janina began to fidget. They were at it again: boring ballet. "We happen to have an even bigger surprise," she announced.

"What?" Ethan jabbed her in the ribs. "*What?*"

But the first of their suitcases came sliding down the chute onto the revolving carousel, and there was no answer until they were in the taxi.

There was a small unnecessary argument about taking a taxi. To Wayne, the occasion obviously demanded one, and he didn't really believe Deedee's concern about expense. It was too easy to rebut: airport bus fare for four wasn't all that cheaper. So what she had to be seeking was the lack of privacy of the bus, the security of not being able to talk intimately.

He was right. She was stalling, but she knew he thought it was for time, and there he was wrong. She simply didn't want half-sentences, loaded ambiguities, in front of the kids; she wanted to get it all out, *had* to get it all out as soon as they were alone. Which couldn't be soon enough for her.

She was so glad he was here, loved his face, yet evaded his eyes. She sat in a corner of the cab, very still, her fingers twitching under her bag, listening to the kids chatter excitedly: Ethan pretending disbelief that Janina hadn't given Wayne ptomaine once, she must've, at least once; then, having gotten a satisfactory rise out of her, switching immediately into the role of tour guide for New York, a city now foreign to Wayne, a city he was ambivalent about despite his enthusiastic punctuations. Easy for Deedee to detect: his expectations and fantasies certainly weren't what hers had been. But what were they, then?

"What's the big surprise?" she blurted out, needing to at least get *that* over with.

A look between Janina and Wayne. "Later," Janina said primly.

"There isn't one!" Ethan taunted.

"Daddy!"

Wayne looked at Deedee. "O.K."

"Well ..." Janina paused dramatically.

"Oh, Jesus." Ethan threw up his hands elaborately. "She's gonna do that number!"

"If you don't want to hear—"

"Come on, Janina," Deedee coaxed.

"Well . . . the Rogers School of Ballet," Janina enunciated with maddening slowness, "has . . . been . . . sold!"

Deedee stared at Wayne. Neither could read the other.

"Dynamite!" Ethan jumped up and down in his seat. "Hey, Dad, one of the guys has a terrific TV agent for kids—"

"Oh, protect me!" Janina fell back against the seat. "TV's gross enough without you blowing the tube!" She laughed at her joke.

"Listen, you creep hick, I've been offered two scholarships!"

"Well, I suppose with Mama's influence—"

"Mom!" Ethan was indignant.

"Whoa!" Wayne cut in. "Back to your corners." He looked at Deedee. "It's a good price, but I didn't close the deal."

"Why not?" Ethan demanded.

"Because I haven't had a chance to talk to your mother about it. O.K.?"

"Oh, sure," Ethan said graciously.

"Besides," Janina informed them, "Daddy has to see what happens in his interviews."

"What interviews?" Deedee asked. "Where? For what?"

"Dance departments at about half a dozen colleges near the city. They sound as though they can't wait to get me." He grinned. "I think they've all gone ballet crazy."

" 'Crazy' is certainly the right word," Janina snorted.

Deedee looked out the window without seeing where they were. Once again she was embarrassed and ashamed at how much he would do for her, how much he would give up for her, *had* given up for her. She found a moment when he was paying the driver and the kids were carrying the bags into the building.

"We have a good life in Oklahoma," she said.

He was about to agree, then checked himself, determined not to start ducking at the outset. "Had," he corrected.

She caught it, was glad, yet didn't quite know how to deal with it. "Well, you like it," she said, not accusing him of anything. "You always have."

"It's always been easier for me. You've always had a tapeworm, and I haven't."

Yes, but I don't anymore, she wanted to say,

but the kids called to hurry, the elevator was there. And as they rode up, she wondered whether it was true, whether she had finally gotten rid of the tapeworm, as he called it, or whether it was still gnawing inside, just a little.

Yes, just a little, because when they entered the apartment and heard the music for *Don Q* coming from the phonograph behind the double doors of Dahkarova's studio, Deedee's first thought was that her daughter was going to dance a role she had never been allowed to do. Well, change didn't come overnight: a woman she knew in Oklahoma City was in her fourteenth year of analysis. One Emma would do her more good. Deedee repressed a giggle: the unspoken "one Emma" had arranged itself in her mind as "one enema." A cleaning out was what she and Wayne needed, but it might be a terrible washout. Nervously, to distract both of them, she managed to open Dahkarova's double doors quietly, just wide enough for Wayne to peek in. It was like looking at history.

A very young girl in characterless practice clothes dances for an old lady sitting in a straight-backed chair. The sunlight coming through the window, flat and sprinkled with dust, belongs to no season; the colorless room, almost devoid of furniture, belongs to no city. Every now and then, the old woman corrects the girl as she herself was corrected by an old woman who in her turn was corrected by another old woman. It is a history where the process is changeless and where the only difference is the individuality of the new pupil. A slight difference, but if it has its own special enchantment, then it enters history.

Dahkarova, like Emma earlier in the day, was watching Emilia for that special difference. The child's technique was secure, but Dahkarova was peering through the dozens of ballerinas dancing in her mind for the nuance personal to Emilia, that was purely Emilia, that would make the difference between a first-rate dancer and a ballerina. Her head nodded to the old recording; she urged Emilia to phrase the music for herself; her hands moved to illustrate, then her arms, then she rose from her chair, took one step, then another, as though she were dancing. And then, though she hardly moved, she was dancing.

Emilia stood still as she saw the change in that remnant of a face as Dahkarova stopped listening to the music and became part of it; saw her change from a dumpy old woman weaving in a dusty haze of sun to a mythical creature in a spotlight, a girl far lovelier and even younger than Emilia herself, a ballerina. She saw why she was Dahkarova, and understood.

In the bedroom that was now theirs, Deedee helped Wayne unpack. The *Don Q* music played faintly down the hall.

"Jesus," Wayne marveled, "the kid's wonderful!"

"She's got two of the best knocking themselves out for her."

"Three." Wayne pointed a finger at Deedee.

She shook her head and smiled. "I ain't been allowed to help. Mama's in the doghouse." An opening, but neither of them dared to take it yet. She hung his blue suit in the closet and went on. "You think she can make it?"

Wayne wasn't sure whether she was sticking to a safe subject or probing to find whether Emilia came first with him. "Will you care if she doesn't?"

"No." Then, thinking back, added, "Not as long as she doesn't."

"Still care that you didn't?" He asked the question casually, but they both stopped unpacking. The silence in the bedroom was louder than the music down the hall.

She was sure he was looking at her, but she was afraid if she turned to face him, she wouldn't be able to get it all out, and she had to, right then. She couldn't wait for tonight.

"Emma said ..." she began, and then, unable to just stand there and say it, took his shirts from the open suitcase on the bed and carried them to the dresser, where she could be very busy putting them one by one in a drawer. "Emma said I married you because I knew I couldn't make it. That's not true. But she also said ... she said that when I got pregnant that first time . . ." It was so difficult, she was almost choking. ". . . with Emilia . . . it was because I wanted to prove to everyone . . . that you weren't gay." She hated the word even more than the suggestion. "That's partly true, Wayne."

O.K. Here it was, scaring the hell out of him.

"I knew that," he said quietly.

She turned to him in surprise. She could see his Adam's apple move as he swallowed.

"I wanted to prove it, too," he said sadly. "So I let you wipe out your whole career."

"But I saddled you with a family to support! You could have been—"

"Me?" He was astonished. "No. Never! Hey . . . I got what I wanted."

"Well," she said, "so did I." It struck her then that it was the truth. Not the whole truth, perhaps, but the basic, the important truth: what you get is what you want. Whatever else she had wanted, she had wanted Wayne most. Not just for the moment, but for the long run, for the life and the children they had together. And looking at him now, seeing in his face the power she had to make him happy, she was grateful that she had wanted what she had. And that she had gotten what she had wanted.

She went running to him, and he, on cue, lifted her high in the air over his graying head. Not as high as he had years ago, but that was because she was heavier now, not because his arms weren't as strong as they used to be. Her eyes were swimming as she smiled down at him, and so were his.

"You always were a good partner," she said.

Neither of them was aware that the music from Dahkarova's studio had stopped. Nor, if they had heard Emilia hurry down the hall or had seen her in the open doorway behind them, would it have occurred to either of them not to let her see Wayne slowly slide Deedee down so they could meet again in a kiss.

Watching, Emilia immediately saw another open door and Yuri and Carolyn; then Wayne holding *her* high in his arms back home. Her adoring smile of anticipation was gone before she turned and slowly walked toward the bedroom she now shared with Janina. Her mother must have told her father about Rosie and it didn't matter to him. He loved her just as much as he always had: Deedee, not her. She was his daughter, his prize pupil; his pride, not his love. She was a fool. Like him.

The bathroom was the only private place in the whole apartment, so she went in and locked the door. Lasting love depended on one person willing to be a fool; she saw that clearly now. What was wrong with her was that she was like her father, not her mother. Her mother was like Yuri.

She searched the mirror over the sink for a physical resemblance to Wayne, instead found the color of her eyes, the determination in them more like Deedee. Well, her mother was a

restless, unusual woman who always wanted
more. Emilia wanted more, too. Not the more
her mother, like Yuri, went after. There was a
better, a finer more, the more Emma had gone
after and had gotten—by not letting anyone get
in the way. Maybe she couldn't be Emma, but
one thing was certain: she was not going to be
a fool, not ever again.

Adelaide had not scheduled an orchestra rehearsal for Emilia's *Don Q.* Although it loomed
as the most enormous event in Emilia's life, and
even though Adelaide hoped it would be
enough of an event to spread the enthusiasm
Emilia had generated in Arnold's ballet, she
was damned if she was going to pay for a
costly rehearsal with an orchestra that was too
damn greedy, anyway, dearie. The conductor—
like Rosie only in his sensitivity to dancers—
came to a rehearsal to set the tempi for Emilia's
variation; he knew the rest from having con-
ducted the pas de deux for Yuri before. Once—
because Yuri had a tight schedule and because
his natural impatience was exacerbated by
Emilia's coolness—Wayne stood in as partner for
Emilia, but not for very long.

Emilia's role in the pas de deux was some-
what coquettish, but her flirtatiousness had a
strong, provocative sensuality that made Wayne
uncomfortably aware of her skin, of the curves
and clefts of her body. He sensed she was
doing it deliberately and became clumsy, be-

gan to sweat, his knees trembled. Peter, who was taking the rehearsal, caught his embarrassment and ended the session by taking Emilia away to the costumer.

Thursday night, Emilia came to the theater very early, with her cassette player, so she could work alone in one of the empty studios. As she watched herself in the mirrored wall, her concentration was so intense that she didn't hear the door open or see Yuri look in. He was wearing an old sweatshirt and the sleek white tights he had worn the day they met in that same mirror. He came into the room and held out his hand to partner her. She stopped moving.

"Why you don't ask me?" His hand was still out.

"Adelaide hates to pay overtime."

"But is no good without me."

The music was still playing. He took her hand and made her dance with him.

"You make too much from Carolyn and me. But I apologize anyway." He grinned. He had a charming grin. "So: can we have supper?"

"I'm busy."

"After supper?"

"Bed."

"O.K." He grinned again, and she stopped dancing. "Emilia. Is joke!"

She had been secure in her coolness, but now her answer told him he was getting to her. "I don't think it's a joke," she said childishly.

Encouraged and exasperated, he abruptly pulled her to him and kissed her. For a moment her lips were hard, pressed tight together; then they relaxed, softened. Slowly, gently, he parted them with his; carefully, delicately brushed them with his tongue, slid the tip of his tongue between her lips, into her eager mouth. Just long enough.

"That is not joke," he said gravely. "Nice?"

She nodded.

"So smile."

He did, but she wouldn't. He put his arm around her, and she held back. To make it easy for her, to make her feel she wasn't giving in, at least not quite yet, he gracefully pulled her to him in the movement of the pas de deux and lifted her, as he would onstage, high in the air above his head. As Wayne had lifted her and then her mother.

"Emilia?" he coaxed, smiling up at her.

His eyes, his hair, all of him was so beautiful; it was so lovely, so exciting to be in his arms again as Emilia rather than only as his partner. She inclined her head a little. Perhaps it was the light, but she saw a glint of triumph in his eyes.

"You're not giving me enough support," she said.

He adjusted their position, and then she did smile. It was the smile of a performer, a ballerina smile. Her head went up, her back arched, her arms and hands reached out regally as though she were onstage in performance.

And then she was.

The best moments in a theater are those when the entire audience becomes one person, transfixed. Such moments are rare and brief, and as electric as they are in the auditorium, they are ten times so on the stage. For there, the performer at last knows power, and thrilled by it, becomes even more powerful by being even more daring. Beyond craft, beyond talent, beyond all the components of art, one element above all is necessary to achieve the power to create that collective thrall: the artist must be a gambler, the risk must be taken. Emilia gambled, she took the risk, and she won.

She knew it, too. As concentrated on what she was doing as Emma had taught her, she nevertheless, as Emma had also taught, kept a small part of herself removed, outside, aware of the people in the vast darkness, of Yuri in his spotlight, of Emilia in hers. She knew when to conserve her energy, when to extend herself, when to dare. She knew when she was all right, when she was good, when she was brilliant. When it was over, she knew they would cheer, knew flowers would rain down from the upper tiers, knew that when Yuri brought her before the front curtain for more bows, fans would run down the aisles with more flowers. She had had enough moments of brilliance; she wasn't there yet, but she was on her way. She knew some of the ovation was because she was young and new, and much of it was for Yuri, who had been even more exciting than usual. But she also knew that he had been better because of her and would want to dance with her again and often. Which was what she wanted.

Out front, to her family, to Emma, to Dahkarova, to everyone, she looked modest and beautiful and touched and thrilled. She *was* thrilled, she couldn't wait to get back onstage again to make them stand up in their seats. Holding a bouquet of dark red roses that, although she didn't know it, had been sent by Emma, she stood onstage waiting to be surrounded. Then she realized the stagehands were changing the backdrop for the next ballet: the evening wasn't over.

So she went to her dressing room, suddenly totally drained, exhausted, gasping for breath. Her feet hurt; there were shooting pains in the muscle of her left calf. In the mirror, she looked thirty: her makeup was running with sweat, her whole body was dripping. And then they burst in: Dahkarova so excited she could only speak in Russian; Janina and Ethan squeezing what wind she had left; and then Wayne, so proud, as proud of her as she had dreamed he would be.

"Thank you," was all he said, but when he kissed her, their tears mingled.

In the doorway, Deedee waited. Wanting to take her daughter in her arms, yet wishing for one flashing moment that she could change places. If it were not for this child, she could have stood in front of that gold curtain, received the flowers, bowed to the applause. She never had, she never would. Never. She had come close, closest of all tonight when her daughter had done it. Her daughter had done it for her, and oh, God, she loved her for it.

Wayne saw her, and turned Emilia slightly, deliberately, so that she saw Deedee, too. Her mother, who had what she had thought she wanted. But she had what her mother wanted and would never get. Slowly she moved from Wayne and went toward Deedee. Like her father, she had difficulty with words. And a kiss could not say it either, would not be enough. She wanted to give Deedee something precious, something that would say everything. Suddenly she knew. Her smile transformed her into a little girl again as she gave her mother the bouquet of roses.

"Dearie, you did it, you did it!" Adelaide burst between them to kiss and hug Emilia. Behind her came Michael and Peter, and then Yuri and Sevilla and Carolyn and God knows who.

The moment was gone, but it was enough for Deedee. She stood in the corridor, cradling the flowers in her arms. Girls in long white tutus hurried by toward the stage. Silently, she wished them well. She wished everybody in the theater well. Emilia's dressing room was getting more crowded, noisier; someone shut the door in Deedee's face. She only smiled and blissfully floated toward the stage. It was very quiet there; the last ballet was about to begin.

Emma was standing in the wings, staring at the stage, her feet spread to form that V. She didn't turn when Deedee came up to her. She knew who it was.

"Pick a feeling," Deedee said softly.

Emma looked at the roses and smiled at Deedee. "Envy. Her life is just beginning. It's not a very long one."

Deedee nodded. "As long as it gives her what she wants."

"Oh, it will." She looked out at the stage, and her eyes were shining. "It will!"

The curtain rose. There was a pale silver glow on the black velvet drop upstage. Down an invisible ramp floated a lovely young girl in a long gossamer tutu: the beginning of *La Bayadère*. The second girl appeared, doing the exact same movements as the first.

Deedee looked at Emma, knowing she was remembering, too, but still not knowing which of them had been the first girl that first time. It didn't matter now, though; only Emilia mattered now.

"Oh, Emma," she said, "if only she knew everything we know!"

Emma turned to her. "It wouldn't matter a damn," she said, and they smiled and turned back to the stage, to watch the procession of girls float down the ramp in long white tutus. The music soared, the lights brightened, and soon the stage was filled with young girls, beginners, all starting out with the same steps, the same hopes, the same innocence, unaware of the short lives that lay ahead.

About the Author

Arthur Laurents lives mainly in a house on the beach in Quogue, Long Island, but goes skiing every winter. His first novel was *The Way We Were,* which he also wrote as a screenplay. Among his other screenplays are *The Snake Pit, Rope,* and *Anastasia.*

The bulk of his writing, however, has been for the theater (where he also directs) and includes such plays as *Home of the Brave, The Time of the Cuckoo, A Clearing in the Woods, Invitation to a March,* and *The Enclave;* and musicals such as *West Side Story, Gypsy, Anyone Can Whistle,* and *Hallelujah, Baby!*

He has long been a member of the Council of The Dramatists Guild.